THE QUEEN'S
NEW YEAR
SECRET

THE QUEEN'S NEW YEAR SECRET

BY

MAISEY YATES

MILLS
BOON

First published in Great Britain 2016
By Mills & Boon, an imprint of HarperCollins*Publishers*
1 London Bridge Street, London, SE1 9GF

Large Print edition 2016

ISBN: 978-0-263-26184-4

Our policy is to use papers that are natural, renewable and recyclable products and made from wood grown in sustainable forests. The logging and manufacturing processes conform to the legal environmental regulations of the country of origin.

Printed and bound in Great Britain
by CPI Antony Rowe, Chippenham, Wiltshire

To my husband.
This has been the best ten years of my life,
and I know the next ten will be even better.

CHAPTER ONE

KAIROS LOOKED ACROSS the bar at the redheaded woman sitting there, her delicate fingertips stroking the stem of her glass, her eyes fixed on him. Her crimson lips were turned up into a smile, the invitation, silent but clear, ringing in the space between them.

She was beautiful. All lush curves and heat. She exuded desire, sexuality. It shimmered over her skin. There was nothing subtle or refined about her. Nothing coy or demure.

He could have her if he wanted. This was the most exclusive and private New Year's Eve party in Petras, and all of the guests would have been vetted carefully. There was no press in attendance. No secret gold diggers looking for a payout. He could have her, with no consequences.

She wouldn't care about the wedding ring on his finger.

He wasn't entirely certain why *he* cared about it anymore. He had no real relationship with his wife. She hadn't even touched him in weeks. Had barely spoken to him in months. Since Christmas she had been particularly cold. It was partly his fault, as she had overheard him saying unflattering things about the state of their union to his younger brother. But it hadn't been anything that wasn't true. Hadn't been anything she didn't already know.

Life would be simpler if he could have the redhead for a night, and just forget about reality. But he didn't want her. The simple, stark truth was as clear as it was inconvenient.

His body wanted nothing to do with voluptuous redheads sitting in bars. It wanted nothing but the cool, blond beauty of his wife, Tabitha. She was the only thing that stoked his fantasies, the one who ignited his imagination.

Too bad the feeling wasn't mutual.

The redhead stood, abandoning her drink, crossing the room and sauntering over to where he sat. The corner of her mouth quirked upward. "You're alone tonight, King Kairos?"

Every night. "The queen wasn't in the mood to go out."

Those lips pursed into a pout. "Is that right?"

"Yes." A lie. He hadn't told Tabitha where he was going tonight. In part, he supposed, to needle her. There was a time when they would have been sure to put in a public appearance during every holiday. When they would have put on a show for the press, and possibly for each other.

Tonight, he hadn't bothered to pretend.

The redhead leaned in, the cloud of perfume breaking through his thoughts and drawing him back to the moment, her lips brushing against his ear, his shirt collar. "I happen to know that our host has a room reserved for guests who would like a bit more...*privacy.*"

There was no ambiguity in that statement.

"You are very bold," he said. "You know I'm married."

"True. But there are rumors about that. As I'm sure you know."

Her words stuck deep into his gut. If the cracks were evident to the public now...

"I have better things to do than read tabloid

reports about my life." He *lived* his tragic marriage. He didn't want to read about it.

She laughed, a husky sound. "I don't. If you want a break from reality, I'm available for a few hours. We can bring in the New Year right."

A break from reality. He was tempted. Not physically. But in a strange, dark way that made his stomach twist, made him feel sick. It was down deep in the part of him that wanted to shake Tabitha's foundation. To make her see him differently. Not as a fixture in her life she could ignore if she wished. But as a man. A man who did not always behave. Who did not always keep his promises. Who would, perhaps, not always be there.

To see if she would react at all. If she cared.

Or if their relationship had well and truly died.

But he did nothing. Nothing but stand, moving away from the woman, and the temptation she represented. "Not tonight, I'm afraid."

She lifted her shoulder. "It could've been fun."

Fun. He wasn't sure he had any idea what that was. There was certainly nothing fun about his line of thinking. "I don't have fun. I have duty."

It wasn't even midnight, and he was ready to leave. Normally, his brother, Andres, would be here, more than willing to swoop in and collect the dejected woman, or any other women who might be hanging around eagerly searching for a *royally* good time.

But now, Andres was married. More than that, Andres was in love. Something Kairos had never thought he'd see. His younger brother completely and totally bound to *one* woman.

Kairos's stomach burned as though there was acid resting in it. He walked out of the club, down the stairs and onto the street where his car was waiting. He got inside and ordered the driver to take him back to the palace. The car wound through the narrow streets, heading out of the city and back toward his home.

Another year come and gone. Another year with no heir. That was why he had commanded Andres to get married in the first place. He was facing the very real possibility that he and Tabitha would not be the ones producing the successor to the throne of Petras.

The duty might well fall to Andres and his wife, Zara.

Five years and he still had no child. Five years and all he had was a wife who might as well be standing on the other side of a chasm, even when they were in the same room.

The car pulled through the massive gates that stood before the palace, then slowly toward the main entrance. Kairos got out without waiting for the driver to assist him, storming inside and up the stairs. He could go to Tabitha's room. Could tell her it was time they tried again for a child. But he wasn't certain he could take her icy reception one more time.

When he was inside her body, pressed against her, skin to skin, it still felt as if she was a thousand miles away from him.

No, he had no desire to engage in that farce, even if it would end in an orgasm. For him.

He didn't want to go to bed yet either.

He made his way up the curved staircase and headed down the hall toward his office. He would have a drink. Alone.

He pushed open the door and paused. The lights

were off, and there was a fire going, casting an orange glow on the surroundings. Sitting in the wingback chair opposite his desk was his wife, her long, slender legs bared by her rather demure dress, her hands folded neatly in her lap. Her expression was neutral, unchanging even as he walked deeper into the room. She didn't smile. She gave almost no indication that she noticed his presence at all. Nothing beyond a slight flicker in her blue eyes, the vague arch of her brow.

The feeling that had been missing when the other woman had approached him tonight licked along his veins like a flame in the hearth. As though it had escaped, wrapping fiery tendrils around him.

He gritted his teeth against the sensation. Against the desire that burned out of his control.

"Were you out?" she asked, her tone as brittle as glass. Cold. Chilling the ardor that had momentarily overtaken him.

He moved toward the bar that was on the far wall. "Was I here, Tabitha?"

"I hardly scoured the castle for you. You may

well have been holed up in one of the many stony nooks."

"If I was not here, or in my room, then it is safe to say that I was out." He picked up the bottle of scotch—already used this evening by his lovely intruder, clearly—and tipped it to the side, measuring a generous amount of liquid into his glass.

"Is that dry tone really necessary? If you were out, just say that you were out, Kairos." She paused then, her keen eyes landing at his neck. "What exactly were you *doing*?" Her tone had morphed from glass to iron in a matter of syllables.

"I was at a party. It is New Year's Eve. That is what people customarily do on the holiday."

"Since when do you go to parties?"

"All too frequently, and you typically accompany me."

"I meant, when do you go to parties for recreational reasons?" She looked down, her jaw clenched tight. "You didn't invite me."

"This wasn't official palace business."

"That is apparent," she said, standing suddenly, reaching out toward his desk and taking hold of the stack of papers that had been resting there, unnoticed by him until that moment.

"Are you angry because you wanted to come?" He had well and truly given up trying to figure his wife out.

"No," she said, "but I am slightly perturbed by the red smudge on your collar."

Were it not for years of practice controlling his responses to things, he might have cursed. He had not thought about the crimson lipstick being left behind after that brief contact. Instead, he stood, keeping his expression blank. "It's nothing."

"I'm sure it is," she said, her words steady, even. "Even if it *isn't* nothing it makes no difference to me."

He was surprised by the impact of that statement. By how hard it hit. He had known she felt that way, he had. It was evident in her every interaction with him. In the way she turned away when he tried to kiss her. In the way she shrank back when he approached her. She was indifferent to him at best, disgusted by him at worst. Of course she wouldn't care if he found solace in the arms of another woman. So long as he wasn't finding it with her. He imagined the only reason she had put up with his touch for so long was out of the hope for children. A hope that faded with each and every day.

She must have given up completely now. A fact he should have realized when she hadn't come to his bed at all in months.

He decided against defending himself. If she didn't care, there was no point discussing it.

"What exactly are you doing here?" he asked. "Drinking my scotch?"

"I have had a bit," she said, wobbling slightly. A break in her composure. Witnessing such a thing was a rarity. Tabitha was a study in control. She always had been. Even back all those years ago when she'd been nothing more than his PA.

"All you have to do is ask the servants and you can have alcohol sent to your own room."

"My own room." She laughed, an unsteady sound. "Sure. Next time I'll do that. But I was actually waiting for you."

"You could have called me."

"Would you have answered the phone?"

The only honest answer to that question wasn't a good one. The truth was, he often ignored phone calls from her when he was busy. They didn't have personal conversations. She never called just to hear his voice, or anything like that. As a result, ignoring her didn't seem all that personal. "I don't know."

She forced a small smile. "You probably wouldn't have."

"Well, I'm here now. What was so important that we had to deal with it near midnight?"

She thrust the papers out, in his direction. For the first time in months, he saw emotion burning from his wife's eyes. "Legal documents."

He looked down at the stack of papers she was holding out, then back at her, unable to process why the hell she would be handing him paper at midnight on New Year's Eve. "Why?"

"Because. I want a divorce."

CHAPTER TWO

TABITHA FELT AS if she was speaking to Kairos from somewhere deep underwater. She imagined the alcohol had helped dull the sensation of the entire evening. From the moment she'd first walked into his empty office with papers in hand, everything had felt slightly surreal. After an hour of waiting for her husband to appear, she had opened a bottle of his favorite scotch and decided to help herself. That had continued as the hours passed.

Then, he had finally shown up, near midnight, an obvious lipstick stain on his collar.

In that moment, the alcohol had been necessary. Without it the impact of that particular blow might have been fatal. She wasn't a fool. She was, after all, in her husband's office, demanding a divorce. She knew their marriage was broken. Irrevocably. He had wanted one thing from her, one thing only, and she had failed to accomplish that task.

The farce was over. There was no point in continuing on.

But she had not expected this. Evidence that her ice block of a husband—dutiful, solicitous and never passionate—had been with someone else. *Recreationally.* For pleasure.

Do you honestly think he waits around when you refuse to admit him into your bed?

Her running inner monologue had teeth tonight. It was also right. She *had* thought that. She had imagined that he was as cold to everyone as he was to her. She had thought that he was—at the very least—a man of honor. She had been prepared to liberate him from her, to liberate them *both*. She hadn't truly believed that he was off playing the part of a single man while still bonded to her by matrimony.

As if your marriage is anything like a real one. As if those vows apply.

"You want a divorce?" The sharpness in his tone penetrated the softness surrounding her and brought her sharply into the moment.

"You heard me the first time."

"I do not understand," he said, his jaw clenched tight, his dark eyes blazing with the kind of emotion she had never seen before.

"You're not a stupid man, Kairos," she said, alcohol making her bold. "I think you know exactly what the words *I want a divorce* mean."

"I do not understand what they mean coming from your lips, Tabitha," he said, his tone uncompromising. "You are my wife. You made promises to me. We have an agreement."

"Yes," she said, "we do. It is not to love, honor and cherish, but rather to present a united front for the country and to produce children. I have been unable to conceive a child, as you are well aware. Why continue on? We aren't happy."

"Since when does happiness come into it?"

Her heart squeezed tight, as though he had grabbed it in his large palm and wrapped his fingers around it. "Some people would say happiness has quite a bit to do with life."

"Those people are not the king and queen of a country. You have no right to leave me," he said, his teeth locked together, his dark eyes burning.

In that moment, it was as though the flame in his eyes met the alcohol in her system. And she exploded.

She reached down, grabbed the tumbler of scotch she'd been drinking from, picked it up and threw it as hard as she could. It missed Kairos neatly, smashing against the wall behind him and leaving a splatter of alcohol and glass behind.

He moved to the side, his expression fierce. "What the hell are you doing?"

She didn't know. She had never done anything like this in her life. She despised this kind of behavior. This emotional, passionate, *ridiculous* behavior. She prized control. That was one of the many reasons she had agreed to marry Kairos. To avoid things like this. She respected him, and—once upon a time—had even enjoyed his company. Their connection had been based on mutual respect, and yes, on his need to find a wife quickly. This kind of thing, shouting and throwing things, had never come into play.

But it was out of her control now. *She* was out of control.

"Oh," she said, feigning surprise, "you noticed me."

Before she could react, he closed the distance between them, wrapping his hand around her wrists and propelling them both backward until her butt connected with the edge of his desk. Rage radiated from him, his face, normally schooled into stone, telegraphing more emotion than she'd seen from him in the past five years.

"You have my attention. So, if that is the aim of this temper tantrum, consider it accomplished."

"This is not a tantrum," she said, her voice vibrating with anger. "This is the result of preparation, careful planning and no small amount of subterfuge. I went to a lawyer. These papers are real. These are not empty threats. This is my decision and it is made."

He reached up, grabbing hold of her chin, holding her face steady and forcing her to meet his gaze. "I was not aware that you had the authority to make decisions concerning both of us."

"That's the beauty of divorce, Kairos. It is an uncoupling. That means I'm free to make independent decisions now."

He reached behind her, gripping her hair, drawing her head back. "Forgive me, my queen, I was not aware that your position in this country superseded my own."

He had never spoken to her this way, had never before touched her like this. She should be angry. Enraged. What she experienced was a different kind of heat altogether. In the very beginning, the promise of this kind of flame had shimmered between them, but over the years it had cooled. To the point that she had been convinced that it had died out. Whatever potential there was had been doused entirely by years of indifference and distance. She had been wrong.

"I was not aware that you had become a dictator."

"Is it not my home? Are you not my wife?"

"Am I? In any meaningful way?" She reached up, grabbing hold of his shirt collar, her thumb resting against the red smudge that marred the white fabric. "This says differently." She pulled hard, the action popping the top button on the shirt, loosening the knot on his gray tie.

His lip curled, his hold on her tightening. "Is

that what you think of me? You think that I was with another woman?"

"The evidence suggests her lips touched your shirt. I would assume they touched other places on your body."

"You think I am a man who would break his vows?" he asked, his voice a growl.

"How would I know? I don't even know you."

"You don't *know* me?" His voice was soft, and all the deadlier for it. "I am your husband."

"Are you? Forgive me. I thought you were simply my stud horse."

He released his hold on her hair, wrapping his arm around her waist and drawing her tightly against his body. He was hot. Hard. Everywhere. The realization caused her heart rate to go into overdrive, her eyes flying wide as she searched his gaze. He was aroused by this. By her. Her circumspect husband who barely made a ripple in the bedspread when he made love to her was aroused by *this*.

"And how can that be, *agape*? When you have not let me near you in almost three months?"

"Was it I who didn't let you near me, or was it you who didn't bother to come to me?"

"A man gets tired of bedding a martyr."

"A woman begins to feel the same," she said, clinging to her anger, trying to ensure that it outstripped the desire that was wrapping itself around her throat, choking her, taking control of her.

He rolled his hips forward, pressing his hardened length against her hip. "Do I feel like a martyr to you?"

"I've always imagined it's the bright future of Petras glowing in your mind's eye that allows you to get it up when you're with me."

He curled the hand pressed onto her back into a fist, taking a handful of material into his grasp and tugging hard. She heard the fabric tear as cool air blew across her now bare back. "Yes," he said, the word dripping with poison. "I am so put upon. Clearly, the sight of your naked body does nothing for me." He pulled her dress down, baring her breasts, covered only by the thin, transparent lace of her bra. "Such a hardship."

He leaned in, tilting his head, pressing a hot,

openmouthed kiss to her neck, the contact so shocking, so unlike anything that had ever passed between them before, she couldn't hold back the sharp cry of shock and pleasure.

She planted her hands on his shoulders, pushing him away. "Who else have you done this with tonight? The woman with the red lipstick? Did you have her like this too? Am I benefiting from the education that she gave you?" He said nothing, he only looked at her, his dark eyes glittering. Her stomach twisted, pain, anger overtaking her. She grabbed hold of the knot on his tie, pulling hard until it came free. She tossed the scrap of silk onto the ground before grabbing hold of his shirt, wrenching it open, buttons scattering over the marble floor.

She stopped, looking at him, her breath coming in short, hard bursts. He was beautiful. He always had been. She'd been struck by his sheer masculine perfection from the moment she'd first seen him. So young, so foolish. Nineteen years old, away from home for the first time, and utterly taken with her new boss.

Of course, she had never imagined that a young

American girl who had come to Petras on a study-abroad program would have a chance with the king of the nation.

Oddly, he was almost more compelling now, in this moment, than he'd been at the first. She had slept with this man for five years. Had seen him naked countless times. The mystery should have been gone. She knew they didn't light the sheets on fire, they never had. It was her, at least she imagined it was. He was her only lover, so she had no one else to compare it with.

Apparently, *he* went out and found women with red lipstick, and things were different. *He* was different.

Rage mingled with the sexual heat rioting through her.

She ran her hands over his chest, the heat of his muscle and skin burning her palms. She should be disgusted by him. She shouldn't want to touch him. Instead, she was insatiable for him. If he had been with another woman, then she would wipe her from his mind. Would erase her touch from his body with her own. She would do what she had not managed to do over the course of five years of marriage. She would make him crave her. Make him desire her.

And then she would leave him.

She leaned forward, parting her lips, scraping her teeth over his chin. He growled, pressing her up against the desk again, pushing her dress the rest of the way down her hips, allowing it to pool on the floor. She didn't recognize him in this moment, didn't recognize herself.

"Did you have someone else?" She asked the question through clenched teeth, as she worked the buckle on his belt, then set about to opening the closure on his dress pants.

He leaned in, claiming her mouth with his, the kiss violent, hard. Bruising. He forced her lips apart, his tongue sliding against hers as he claimed her, deep and uncompromising. She let the rage of the unanswered question simmer between them, stoking the flame of her desire.

He took hold of the front of her bra, pulling it down, revealing her breasts. He bent his head, taking one tightened bud into his mouth and sucking hard. She gasped, threading her fingers through his hair, holding him tightly against her.

She wanted to punish him, for tonight, for the past five years. She didn't know what else to do but to punish him with her desire. Desire she had kept long hidden. Until tonight, they had never so much as yelled at one another. This was more passion than either of them had ever shown.

Perhaps it was the same for him. An outlet for his anger. A punishment. But it was one she would gladly allow herself to be subjected to. Because for all that she knew she would walk away from this damaged, destroyed, she knew that he would not walk away from it unscathed either.

He shifted, blazing a path between her breasts with the flat of his tongue, his teeth grazing her neck, her jaw, before he finally claimed her mouth again. He reached between them, freeing his erection, so hot and hard against her skin.

She planted her hands on his shoulders, pushing them beneath the fabric of his shirt, scraping her fingernails along his flesh, relishing the harsh sound that he made in response. He tightened his hold on her, setting her up on the surface of his desk, moving to stand between her spread thighs. He pressed his arousal against her slick, sensitive skin, still covered by her flimsy panties, rolling his hips, sending a shock wave of pleasure through her body.

"Answer me," she said, digging her fingernails more deeply into his shoulders.

He shifted, sliding his hands down beneath the fabric of her underwear, his fingertips grazing the sensitized bundle of nerves there. "You want to know if I did this to another woman?" His words were rough, jagged. He hooked his finger around the edge of her panties, drawing them to the side, pressing the head of his shaft to the entrance of her body. "You want to know if I did *this* with another woman?"

"Just answer the question," she hissed.

"I think you would have me either way."

Her face heated, humiliation pouring through her. He was right. In this moment, she would be hard-pressed to deny him or her body anything. "Is that why you won't tell me? For fear I'll turn you away?"

"I'm used to you turning me away, Tabitha. Why should I waste a moment of regret over it now?"

She slid her hands down his well-muscled back,

cupping his ass. "You would regret this." She rolled her hips forward, taking him deeper inside her body, just another inch. "You would regret not finishing this."

"No," he said, and for a moment, her heart sank. For a moment, she thought he meant he would not regret losing out on this moment between them. For a moment, she thought that yet again, she was alone in what she was experiencing. "I was not with anyone else. I did not touch another woman. She propositioned me. She whispered in my ear. I said no."

Then he kissed her before driving deep into her body. She gasped, and he took advantage, tasting her deeply as he flexed his hips again, withdrawing slightly before seating himself fully inside her again.

A rough groan escaped her lips, white-hot pleasure streaking through her. She clung more tightly to him, wrapping her legs around his back, urging him on. Urging him to take it harder, faster. She had no patience. Had no more desire in her to cultivate an effort to take things slow, to practice restraint. There was nothing but him, nothing but this. Nothing but years of anger, frustration, being uncovered as their inhibitions were stripped away layer by layer, with each thrust of his body into hers.

A shudder wracked his large frame, pleasure stealing his control. She relished that. Took pride in it. But it wasn't enough. She wanted to give him pleasure, she absolutely did. Wanted him to think of this later, to regret all of the years when they didn't have this. To look back on this one moment and ache forever. For the rest of his days, no matter whom he married down the road. Whoever came after her, whether she bore children for him or not, Tabitha wanted him to always think of her.

But pleasure wasn't enough. She wanted to punish him too. She dug her fingernails deep into his skin and he growled, angling his head and biting her neck, the action not gentle at all, painful. He flexed his hips, his body making contact with that sensitive bundle of nerves, and she knew that he was trying to do the same to her that she was doing to him. As if she deserved his wrath. As if she deserved his belated, angry gift of pleasure. *He* was the one who had done this to them. This was his fault.

She tightened her grip on him, met his every thrust with a push from her own body, met his each and every growl with one of her own. She had been passive for too long. The perfect wife who could never be perfect enough. So why bother? Why not just break it all?

She closed her eyes tightly, fusing her lips to his, kissing him with all of the rage, desire and regret that she had inside of her, the action pushing them both over the edge. It had been so long. So very long. Not just since she had been with him, but since she had found pleasure in his arms. So many months of coming together when she was at the optimum place in her cycle, perfunctory couplings that meant nothing and felt like less than nothing.

This was different than anything that had come before it. He'd given her orgasms before, but nothing like this. Nothing this all-consuming. Nothing this altering. This devastating. This was like a completely different experience. She was falling in the dark with no way of knowing when she would hit the bottom. All she knew was that she would. And when she did, it would be painful beyond anything she had ever known before. But for now, she was simply falling, with him.

The last time. The last moment they would ever be together.

She wanted to weep. With the devastation of it. With the triumph of it. This was it for them. The final nail in the coffin of their marriage. How she desperately needed it. How she resented it. She wanted to transport herself somewhere in the future. Years from now, maybe. To a time when she'd already healed from the wounds that would be left behind after they separated. A moment in time when she would have already learned to be Just Tabitha again, and not Tabitha, Queen of Petras, wife of Kairos. But Tabitha, on her own.

At the same time, she wanted to stay in this moment. Forever. She wanted to hold on to him forever and never let go.

Which was why she needed to let go. She so badly needed to let go.

The pleasure stretched on, an onslaught of waves that never ceased and she couldn't catch her breath. Couldn't think beyond what he made her feel. It wasn't fair. It just wasn't fair. Why was this happening now? She had always believed this was there between them, that it could be unlocked, somehow, but they had never found it. Not until this moment. This very last moment.

Finally the storm subsided, leaving her spent, exhausted. Smashed against the rock. She was wrung out. She had nothing left in her to give. No more rage. No more desire. Nothing but an endless sadness for what her life had become. She looked at the man still holding her tightly. The man still inside her body. The man she had made vows to.

A man who was a stranger, half a decade after she'd first made love to him.

"I hate you," she said, the words a hoarse whisper that shocked even herself. A tear slid down her cheek and she didn't bother to wipe it away. "For every one of the past five years you have wasted, I hate you. For being my husband but never really being my husband. I hate you for that too. For not giving me a baby. For making me want you even when I hate you."

He pushed away from her, his gaze dark. "Let me guess, you hate me for that too."

"I do. But the good thing is, that after today, we won't have to see each other."

"Oh, I think not, *agape*. I think we will have to see each other a great many times after today. A royal divorce is going to be complicated. There will be press. There will be many days in court—"

"We signed a prenuptial agreement. I remember the terms well. I don't get anything. That's fine. I've had quite enough from you."

He made no move to dress, made no move to collect her clothes. And he didn't look away as she bent to gather them, pulling them on as quickly as possible, internally shrinking away from his gaze. Finally, she was dressed. It was done. It was over.

She made her way toward the door on unsteady legs, everything inside her unsteady, rolling like the sea.

"Tabitha," he said, his voice rough, "I want you to know that I don't hate you."

"You don't?" She turned to face him, her eyes

meeting with his unreadable face. As immovable as stone.

He shook his head slowly, his eyes never leaving hers. "No. I feel…" He paused for a moment. "I feel nothing."

She felt as though he had stabbed her directly in the heart. Anguish replaced any of the pleasure, any of the satisfaction that had been there before. He felt *nothing*. Even in this moment he felt nothing.

The rage was back then, spurring her on, keeping her from falling over. "You just screwed me on your desk," she said, "I would have thought that might have made you feel something."

She was all false bravado. It was either that or burst into tears.

His expression remained bland. "You're hardly the first woman I've had on a desk."

She swallowed hard, blinking back more tears. She had made the right choice. She knew she had. Had he yelled at her, had he screamed, had he said that he hated her too, she might have wondered. But those black, flat, soulless eyes didn't lie. He felt nothing. He was indifferent, even in this moment.

Tabitha had heard it said that hate was like murder. But she knew differently. It was indifference that killed. And with his, Kairos had left her mortally wounded.

"I wish you luck in your search for a more suitable wife, Your Highness," she said.

Then she walked out of the door, out of his life.

CHAPTER THREE

"WHERE IS YOUR WIFE, Kairos?"

Prince Andres, Kairos's younger reformed rake of a brother, walked into Kairos's office. There was still glass on the floor from where Tabitha had shattered it two days ago. Still a dark stain where the scotch had splashed itself over the wallpaper.

All of it shouted the story of what had happened the night Tabitha had left. At least, it shouted at Kairos. Every time he walked in.

It was nearly as loud as his damned conscience.

I feel nothing.

A lie. Of course it was a lie. She had stripped him down. Reduced him to nothing more than need, desperate, clawing need.

Another woman walking away from him. Threatening to leave him there alone. Empty.

While his pride bled out of him, leaving him with nothing.

He couldn't allow that, not again. So he'd said he felt nothing. And now she was gone.

"Why? What have you heard?" Kairos asked, not bothering to explain the glass, even when Andres's eyes connected with the mess.

"Nothing much. Zara tells me Tabitha called to see if I could find out if you were using your penthouse anytime soon. I wondered why on earth my brother's wife would be stooping to subterfuge to find out the actions of her own husband."

Kairos ground his teeth together, his eyes on the shards of glass.

I feel nothing for you.

If only that were true. He was…he didn't even know what to call the emotions rioting through him. Emotions were…weak and soft in his estimation, and that was not what he felt.

He was beyond rage. Beyond betrayal. She was his wife. He had brought her up from the lowest of positions, made her a queen, and she had the audacity to betray him.

"No explanation, Kairos?"

Kairos looked up at his brother. "She probably wants to go shopping without fear of retribution."

"Right. Are the coffers of Petras so empty she has to worry about your wrath? Or is her shoe closet merely so full."

Kairos had no idea what her closet looked like. He never looked farther than her bed when he was in her room. "She left me," he said, his tone hard, the words like acid on his tongue.

Andres had the decency to look shocked. Surprising, because Andres was rarely shocked and he was never decent. "Tabitha *left* you?"

"Yes," he ground out.

"Tabitha, who barely frowns in public for fear it might ignite a scandal?"

Kairos dragged his hand over his face. "That is the only Tabitha I know of."

"I don't believe it."

"Neither do I," Kairos said, his voice a growl.

He paced across the office, to the place where the remains of that glass of scotch rested. It reminded him of the remnants left behind after an

accident on the highway. One of the many simi-
larities the past few days bore to a car crash.

I hate you.

He closed his eyes against the pain that lashed
at him. What had he done to make his wife hate
him? Had he not given her everything?

A baby. She wanted a baby.

Yes, he had failed her there. But dammit all,
he'd given her a *palace*. Some women couldn't
be pleased.

"What the hell did you do?"

"I was perhaps too generous," Kairos said, his
tone hard. "I gave her too much freedom. Perhaps the weight of her diamond-encrusted crown
was a bit heavy."

"You don't know," Andres said, his tone in-
credulous.

"Of course I bloody don't. I had no idea she
was unhappy." The lie was heavy on his chest.

You knew. You didn't know how to fix it.

"I know I haven't been married very long…"

"A week, Andres. If you begin handing out
marital advice before the ink is dry on your li-
cense, I will reopen the dungeons just for you."

"Perhaps if you'd opened the dungeons for Tabitha she wouldn't have left you."

"I am not going to keep my own wife prisoner." But dear God, it was tempting.

Andres arched a brow. "That isn't what I meant."

Heat streaked along Kairos's veins, and he thought again of that last night here in his office. Of the way she'd felt in his arms. His cool ice queen suddenly transformed into a living flame…

I hate you.

"We do not have that sort of relationship," Kairos said, his voice stiff.

Andres chuckled, the sound grating against Kairos's nerves. "Maybe that's your problem."

"Everything is not about sex."

Andres shrugged. "It absolutely is. But you may cling to your illusions if you must."

"What do you want, Andres?"

"To see if you're okay."

He spread his arms wide. "Am I dead and buried?"

His brother arched a brow. "No. But your wife is gone."

Kairos gritted his teeth. "And?"

"Do you intend to get a new one?"

He would have to. There was no other alternative. Though the prospect filled him with nothing but dread. Still, even now, he wanted no one else. No one but Tabitha.

And now that he'd tasted the heat that had always shimmered between them as a tantalizing promise, never before fulfilled…

Forgetting her would not be so easy.

"I do not want a new one," he said.

"Then you have to go and claim the old one, I suppose."

Kairos offered his brother a glare. "Worry about your life, I'll worry about mine." He paused for a moment, staring again at that pile of broken glass. The only thing that remained of his marriage. "I will not hold her prisoner. If Tabitha wants a divorce, she can have her damn divorce."

Tabitha hadn't seen Kairos in four weeks. Four weeks of staring at blank spaces, eyes dry, unable to find any tears. She hadn't cried. Not since that single tear had fallen in his office. Not since she'd told him how much she hated him—and meant it—with every piece of herself. She had not cried.

Why would you cry for a husband that you hated? Why would you cry for a husband who felt nothing for you?

It made no sense. And so, she hadn't cried. Tabitha was nothing if not sensible. Even when she came to divorce, it seemed.

She was slightly less sensible when it came to other things. Which was why it had taken her a full week of being late for her to make her way to the doctor. She had no choice but to use the doctor she had always used. She didn't want to, didn't want to be at risk by going to a doctor who was employed by the royal family. But her only other alternative was going to one she had no relationship with. One she had no trust in at all. News of her and Kairos's divorce had already hit the papers, and it was headline news. If she went to an ob-gyn now, everything would explode. She couldn't risk it. So she was risking this. She swallowed hard, her hands shaking as she sat on the exam table. Her blood had already been drawn, and now she was just waiting for the results.

She had waited so long to come to the doctor because she was often late. Her period never started on time. For years upon years every time she had been late she'd held out hope. Hope that this time it wasn't just her cycle being fickle. Hope that it might actually be a baby.

It was never a baby. *Never.*

But it had been a full week, and still nothing. And she couldn't overlook the fact that she and Kairos had had unprotected sex.

Nothing unusual there, though. They always had. For five years they'd had unprotected sex, and there had been no baby. The universe was not that cruel. How could God ignore her prayers for five long years, and answer them at the worst possible moment?

It couldn't be. It *couldn't* be.

For the first time, when the doctor walked back into the room, her expression unreadable, Tabitha hoped for the *no*. She needed it. Needed to hear that the test was negative.

She knew now that she couldn't live with

Kairos. It was confirmed. She couldn't make it work with him. He didn't care for her. And she… she felt far too much for him. She could not live like that. She simply couldn't.

"Queen Tabitha," Dr. Anderson said, her words slow. "I had hoped that King Kairos might have accompanied you today."

"If you read the paper at all, then you know that he and I are going through a divorce. I saw no reason to include him in this visit." The doctor looked down and Tabitha's stomach sank. A *no* was an easy answer to give. A *no* certainly didn't require Kairos's presence.

"Yes, I do know about the divorce," the doctor said. "All members of royal staff had been briefed, of course."

"Then you know why he isn't here."

"Forgive me for asking, my queen," the doctor said. "But if you are in fact carrying a child, is it his?"

"If I am? You've seen the test results. Don't play this game with me. Do not play games with me. I've had enough."

"It's just that…"

"This is *my* test. It has nothing to do with him. My entire life does not revolve around *him*." Tabitha knew she was beginning to get a bit hysterical. "I left him. I left him so that he wasn't at the center of everything I did. We don't need to bring him into this."

"The test is positive, my queen. I feel that under other circumstances congratulations would be in order," Dr. Anderson said, her tone void of expression.

Before this, before the divorce proceedings, Dr. Anderson had always been friendly, warm. She was decidedly cool now.

A King Kairos loyalist, clearly. But Dr. Anderson didn't have to live with him.

"Oh." Tabitha felt light-headed. She felt like she was going to collapse. She was thankful for the table she was seated on. Had she been standing, she would have slipped from consciousness immediately.

"Based on the dates you have given me I would estimate that you are…"

"I know exactly how far along I am," Tabitha said.

Flashes of that night burst into her mind's eye.

Kairos putting her up on the desk, thrusting into her hard and fast. Spilling himself inside of her as they both lost themselves to their pleasure. Yes, there was no doubt in her mind as to when she had conceived. January 1.

The beginning of the New Year. What was supposed to be the start of her new beginning.

And all she had was a chain shackling her to Kairos now that she had finally decided to walk out the door and take her freedom.

Of course this was happening now. When she'd released hold of her control. Her inhibitions. There were reasons she'd kept herself on a short leash for so many years. She'd always suspected she couldn't be trusted. That she would break things if she was ever allowed to act without careful thought and consideration.

She'd been right to distrust herself.

She balled her hands into fists and pressed them against her eyes.

"Are you all right?" Dr. Anderson asked.

"Does it look like I'm all right?" Tabitha asked. "It's only that...*is* it the king's baby?"

Rage fired through Tabitha then. "It is *my* baby. That's about all I can process at the moment."

Dr. Anderson hesitated. "It's only that I want to be certain that I didn't overstep."

As those words left the doctor's mouth, the door to the exam room burst open. Tabitha looked up, her heart slamming hard against her sternum. There was Kairos. Standing in the doorway, looking like a fallen angel, rage emanating from him.

"Leave us," he said to the doctor.

"Of course, Your Highness."

The doctor scurried out of the room, eagerly doing Kairos's bidding. Tabitha could only sit there, dazed. She supposed that there was no such thing as doctor-patient confidentiality when the king was involved.

She turned to face her nearly ex-husband—who was looking at her as though she were the lowest and vilest of creatures. As if he had any right. As if he had the right to judge her. After what he had said. After what he had done.

"What's the matter, Kairos?" she asked, schooling her expression into one of absolute calm and stillness. It was her specialty. After years of hiding her true feelings behind a mask for public consumption, she went about it with as much ease as breathing.

"It seems I'm about to be a father." He moved nearer to her, his dark eyes blazing. Any blankness, any calm he had presented the night she had left him standing in his office was gone now. He was all emotion now. He was vibrating with it.

"You're making an awfully big assumption."

He slammed his hands down on the counter by the exam table. "Do not toy with me, Tabitha. We both know it's my child."

"Except that *you* don't. Because you can't know that. You haven't seen me in weeks. I didn't go to your bed for months before our last time together." Heartbreak made her cruel. She'd had no idea. She'd never been heartbroken before him.

"I am the only man you have ever been with. You and I both know that. You were a virgin when I had you the first time. I sincerely doubt you went out and found the first lover available to you just after leaving my arms."

She swallowed hard, her hands trembling. "You

say that as though you know me. We both know that you don't. We both know that you feel nothing for me."

"In this moment, I find I feel quite a lot."

"I've only just found out. It isn't as though I was keeping a secret from you. Where exactly do you get off coming in here, playing the part of caveman?"

"You were going to keep it from me. The doctor called me. If you knew you were coming to the doctor to get a pregnancy test, why didn't you include me?"

"Because," she said, looking at the wall beyond him, "that's the beauty of divorce. I don't have to include you in my life. I get to go on as an individual. Not as one half of the world's most dysfunctional couple. I would have told you. I was hardly going to keep this from you. If for no other reason than that the press would never let me."

"How very honorable of you. You would let me in on my impending fatherhood based on what the media would allow you to keep secret. Tell me, would you allow them to announce it to me via headline?"

"That sounds about right considering the level of communication we've always had. Honestly, I haven't much noticed the absence of you in the past four weeks. It was pretty much standard to our entire marriage. Sex once a month with no talking in between."

"Still your poisonous tongue for a moment, my queen. We have a serious issue to deal with here."

"There is no *issue*," she said, her hand going protectively to her stomach. "And there is no *dealing* with it. What's done is done."

"What exactly did you think I was suggesting?" His dark features contorted with horror. With anger. "You cannot seriously think I would suggest you get rid of our child. Just because you and I are experiencing difficult circumstances at the moment—"

"No. That isn't what I thought you meant. And what do you mean difficult circumstances? We are not undergoing difficult circumstances. If anything, we're experiencing some of the best circumstances we've had in years. We aren't together anymore, Kairos. That's what we both need."

"Not now. There will be no discussion of it."

She stood up, feeling dizzy. "The hell there won't be. I am not your property. I can divorce you if I choose, discussion or not."

"Can you? I am king of Petras."

"And I am an American citizen."

"In addition to being a citizen of Petras."

"I will happily chuck my Petran passport into the river. As long as it will get you off my back."

"We are not having this discussion here," he said through clenched teeth. "Get dressed. We're leaving."

"I have a car."

"Oh, yes, my driver that you're still using. From the house that I own that you are currently living in."

"I will sort things out later," she said, stinging heat lashing her cheekbones. It was humiliating to have him bring up the fact she was dependent on him to not be homeless at the moment. Particularly since she had made such a big deal out of knowing she would get nothing from him after the divorce. But still, he wasn't using his apartment in town, nor was he using the car and driver that were headquartered there. So he could hardly deny her the use of them. Well, he *could*. But he wasn't, so she was taking advantage.

"Oh, I sent your driver home. The only driver currently here is mine. You are leaving with me. Now."

He stood there, his arms folded across his broad chest, his dark eyes glued to her.

"Don't look at me. I have to get dressed."

"It is nothing I haven't seen, *agape*."

She treated him to her iciest glare. "Rarely."

The biting word hung between them and she felt some guilt over it. Truly, the state of their sex life was partly her fault. If not mostly her fault. But having him touch her out of duty… It had certainly started to wear on her.

Eventually, it was just easier to lie back and think of Petras. To close her eyes and think of other things. Hope that it would be over quickly. To not allow herself to feel a connection with him. To shut walls around her heart, and around her body. The less she felt during sex, the less pain she felt when it was over. The less disappointment each time he got up and left immediately after, each time the pregnancy test was negative. The less distress she felt over the fact that any intimacy between them was all for the purpose of producing a child. That it was completely void of any kind of emotion between the two of them.

Yes, the fast, disappointing sex in the dark was mainly her fault.

"As you wish, my queen." He turned away from her, his broad back filling her vision. And, damn him, she felt bad. Guilty. He did *not* deserve her guilt.

She kept her eyes on him as she stripped off the hospital gown she was wearing. On the way the perfectly cut lines of his suit molded to his physique. He was a handsome man. There was no denying it. He was also a bastard.

She finished dressing, then cleared her throat.

Kairos turned, the fierceness in his expression wavering for a moment. An emotion there that she couldn't quite put a name to.

"Let's go," he said.

"Where are you taking me?"

"To the palace." He hesitated. "We have some things to discuss."

"I don't want to discuss this right now. I've only just found out I'm pregnant. I believe you had to know before I did."

"You at least had a suspicion."

"You think that makes it easier? Do you think that makes any of this…?" Her voice broke, her entire body shaking. "I should not be devastated in this moment. I hate you for this too. I was supposed to be happy when I finally conceived. You've stolen that for me."

"Who stole it, Tabitha? I was not the one who asked for a divorce."

"Maybe not. But you made your feelings for me perfectly clear. It's poison now, already working its way through my system. You can't fix it."

He said nothing as they walked out of the exam room and continued down the long vacant hallway toward a back entrance. His car was waiting there, not one driven by a chauffeur. One of his sports cars that he got great enjoyment out of driving.

He was a low-key man, her husband. Responsible, levelheaded. Serious.

But he liked cars. And he very much enjoyed

driving them. Much too fast for her taste. But he never asked her opinion.

"I'm not especially in the mood to deal with your Formula 1 fantasies," she said, crossing her arms and tapping her foot, giving him her best withering expression.

"Funny. I'm not particularly in the mood to put up with your attitude, and yet, here we are."

"You have earned every bit of my attitude, Your Highness."

"So angry with me, Tabitha, when you spent so many years with so little to say."

"What *have* I said, my lord?"

He made a scoffing sound in the back of his throat. "My lord. As if you are ever so deferential."

She arched her brow. "As if you ever deserved it." She breezed past him and got inside the car, slamming the door shut behind her and setting about to buckling her seat belt while he got in and started the engine.

"What happened, Tabitha? *What happened?*"

"There was nothing. Like you said. Nothing. And I can't live that way anymore."

"You're having my baby. I don't see you have an option now. Clearly the divorce is off."

He revved the engine, pressing the gas and pulling the car away from the curb.

"The divorce is no such thing," she said, panic clawing at her insides. "The divorce is absolutely on. You might be royalty, but you can't pull endless weight with me. I am not simply another subject in your country. I have rights."

"Oh, really? And with what money will you hire a lawyer to defend those rights? Everything you have is mine, Tabitha, and we both know it."

"I will find a way." She didn't know if she would. He wasn't wrong. She was nothing. Nothing from nowhere. She had climbed her way up from the bottom. From a poor household on the wrong side of the tracks with parents who would spend every night screaming at each other, throwing things. Her mother hurling heavy objects at her stepfather's head whenever the mood struck her.

And that was before everything had gone horribly wrong.

There had been no money in her household.

Not enough food. All there had been was anger. And that was an endless well. One that her parents drew from at every possible opportunity. That was her legacy. It was all she had. It was why she had vowed to find something different for herself. Something better.

What she had found was that sometimes everything that filled the quiet spaces, everything that went unsaid, was more cutting, more painful than a dinner plate being hurled at your head.

Kairos said nothing but simply kept driving. It took a while for her to realize they weren't heading back to the palace, but when she did, a cold sense of dread filled her. She realized then that she honestly couldn't predict what he might be doing. Because she didn't know him. Five years she had been married to this man and she knew even less about him today than she had on the day they had married. Impossible, seemingly.

She'd spent three years as his PA prior to them getting engaged and married. Three years where she had cultivated a silly, childish crush on him. He had smiled easier then, laughed with her sometimes.

But that was before his father had died. Before the weight of the nation had fallen on his shoulders. Before his arranged engagement was destroyed by his impetuous younger brother. Before he had been forced to take on a replacement wife that he had never wanted, much less loved.

Those years spent as his PA had been like standing on the outside of a forest. She had looked on him and thought, *I recognize him. He's a forest.* Being his wife was like walking through it. Discovering new dangers, discovering that it was so dark, she could barely see in front of her. Discovering she had no idea where the trees might end, and where she might find her freedom. Yes, the deeper she walked, the less she knew.

"You aren't planning on driving your car into a river or something dramatic, are you?" she asked, only half joking.

"Don't be silly. We spent years trying for an heir, I'm not going to compromise anything now that we have one on the way."

"Oh, but otherwise you would be aiming for a cliff. Good to know."

"And leave Andres to rule? Don't be ridiculous."

It occurred to her suddenly, exactly where they were heading. Unease stole over her, her scalp prickling. "What are you planning?"

"Me? Perhaps I'm not planning anything. Perhaps I'm being spontaneous."

"I don't believe that."

"You're so convinced that I don't know you, and yet, you think you know me, *agape*? How fair is that?"

She didn't think she knew him. But she wasn't about to admit that now. "You're a man, Kairos. Moreover, you're a distinctly predictable one."

"If I cared about your opinion at all I would be tempted to feel wounded. Alas, I don't."

He turned onto the private airfield used by the royal family and her heart sank. Her suspicions were very much confirmed. "What is it you think you're doing?"

"Oh, I don't think I'm doing anything. This is the situation, my darling bride, either you come with me now or we do this here in Petras."

"Do what, exactly?"

"Come to an agreement on exactly what we will do now that we are to be parents. And by come to an agreement, I mean what I will decide. Do not forget that I am the king. Whatever laws might govern the rest of the people do not apply to me."

Rage filled her, flooded her. "Since when? You've never been the most flexible of men, but you've never been a dictator."

"I've never been a father before either. Neither have I ever been in the position of having my wife threaten to leave me."

"I didn't threaten to leave you, Kairos. I left you. There is a difference."

"Regardless. Come with me, and we will have a discussion. If you refuse, then I will ensure that I get full custody of our child, and you will never see him. I give you my word on that. And unlike you, when I make a vow, I keep it."

CHAPTER FOUR

KAIROS LOOKED AT his wife, who was seated across the cabin from him on his private plane. He had a feeling she was plotting his death. Fortunately, Tabitha was quite petite or he might harbor some concern over her having access to any cutlery. At this point, he doubted she would hesitate to attempt to take him out with her fork. In many ways, he couldn't blame her. But he had to guard his own self-interest, and guard it he would.

There was no room to be soft in this.

She was having his baby. An heir. *Finally.*

At any other time this would have been a cause for celebration. The completion of his duty in many ways. A fulfillment of deathbed promises made to a father he'd never quite pleased during his life.

The moment he'd found out, the only thought

he had was how he could capture her. Keep her with him. He had no idea what he was going to do beyond that. But he had managed to get her on the plane, even though it had taken threats. Now, they were en route to his private island off the coast of Greece. The villa there had always been used by the royal family of Petras for vacations. Kairos had never taken Tabitha there. He had not been on a vacation since he had taken her as his wife.

Of course, this was no vacation. Some might call it a kidnapping. But he was king. So he imagined he could classify it as some kind of political detention. She was, after all, carrying the heir to the throne of Petras. If she were to leave, it would be kidnapping on her end.

At least, that's how he was justifying things. And he was king. The amount of people he had to justify his actions to was limited to one. Himself.

She didn't look angry. She looked as smooth and unruffled as ever. Her hands were folded in her lap, her legs crossed at the ankles, her lovely neck craned as she looked out the window. She managed to appear both neutral and haughty, a feat he had only ever seen managed by Tabitha.

Years of routine. A marriage so mundane he could go days without looking at her. Even if they were in the same room. He would look in her direction, but, he realized, never truly look at her. It was easy sometimes to go a full week without words passing directly between them. Communication with a phone or servant as the go-between.

And in the space of the past four weeks everything had changed. She had asked for a divorce. Then he'd torn her clothes off and taken her like a rutting animal. Now there was a baby.

The past four weeks contained more than the past half decade they'd spent as husband and wife. He was having a difficult time wrapping his head around it. Around who he had become in her arms in those moments in his office. He was angry. Enraged that she would walk away from him after all he had done for her. Enraged that half-formed fantasies he had barely let himself dream would never come to be.

He had imagined they would be married all

of their lives. He had never imagined she would end it.

"Are you quite comfortable?" he asked, because he could think of nothing else to say and he had grown quite uncomfortable with his role as uncivilized beast and the little play they were currently acting out.

He was the responsible one. He'd never acted out, not once in his life. His father had impressed the weight of the crown upon him at an early age, and Kairos had always taken it seriously. He had seen the consequences of what happened when one did not. Had had it ingrained in him.

Control was everything. Duty. Honor. Sacrifice.

He was surprised how easily he had cast it off the moment his wife had handed him divorce papers.

And so, he was attempting to reclaim it.

As you kidnap her. Brilliant.

"Yes," she said, her tone brittle. "Very. But then, I don't have to tell you your private plane is luxurious. You already know."

"Indeed."

"How long had I been working for you the first time we flew on this plane?"

"A couple of months, surely," he said, as though he didn't remember it clearly. He did. There was something so charming and guileless about her reaction to the private aircraft. It had stood in stark contrast to the response of his fiancée at the time, Francesca.

He had noticed it then, as he compared the two women unfavorably. Francesca was, of course, eminently suitable to be a royal bride. That was why he had selected her. Love had never come into play. She had been raised in an aristocratic family, trained to be the wife of a political leader from an early age.

Of course, it had all blown up in his face when she had slept with his brother. That might not have bothered him so much, had she not done it quite so publicly. Not that she had intended for it to go public. Ruining her chances of becoming the queen of Petras had not been the plan. That much he knew. Still, a video had surfaced of the two of them together, and that did it for their wedding.

He needed to find a wife to fill in for the royal wedding that was already planned, and quickly. And so, he had selected Tabitha to be his bride. A logical decision. An acceptable flesh-and-blood woman.

Perhaps all women were destined to go crazy at some point in their lives. His mother certainly had. Walking out on her husband and children in the dead of night, never resurfacing again. Francesca most certainly had when she'd compromised her position as queen simply so she could experience some pleasure with Andres. Obviously, Tabitha was the newest victim of the craze.

Or maybe it's you.

He gritted his teeth.

"I was impressed with it then," she said. "I remain impressed. I am less impressed with the fact that you hijacked my person."

"It was a hard-line negotiation, not a hijacking. Surely you see the difference."

"The end result is the same to me, so why should I care about semantics?"

"You were quite impressed with the plane," he said, his voice hard, "as I recall."

"Don't tell me you remember."

"Of course I remember. You were very young. Wide-eyed about everything you encountered here in Petras. Especially everything concerning the royal family and the palace. I had a fair idea about your background, because of course I screened you before hiring you. I knew you came from a modest upbringing."

"That's a generous way of putting it."

"Impoverished, then. Yes, I knew. But you were bright, and you were certainly the best person for the job. You were motivated, in part because of your past. I thought, possibly more driven than any of the other candidates to succeed."

"Are these the same thoughts you had when you selected me to be your wife?"

He could sense the layers hidden beneath the question, but couldn't guess what they were. "I also knew you," he said.

She made a scoffing sound, uncrossed her legs, then recrossed them the opposite direction, annoyance emanating from her in a wave. "Oh. You *knew* me. As in, were acquainted with me. How very romantic."

"Did I ever promise you romance, Tabitha?" She said nothing, her glare glacial now. "No. I did not. I told you that I would stay faithful to you, and I have. I told you that I would be loyal to you, which I have also done. That I would do my duty to God, country and to you. I have done all of that, to a satisfactory degree, many would say. You were the one who decided it wasn't enough."

Righteous anger burned through him. He had not lied to her. He had not told her he would give hearts, flowers or any frilly symbol of weak emotion. He had pledged commitment.

She seemed to have no concept of that at all. He would never have taken her for being so faithless. He had thought she was like him. Had thought she was logical. Had thought that she understood sacrifice. That duty and honor superseded emotion.

"A theoretical marriage is a lot different than actual marriage. I can hardly be held to assumptions I made before I had ever had a…a relationship."

"Certainly you can. Everyone makes vows before they marry. For the most part, they have never made such vows before."

"And sometimes marriages end. Because in spite of the best intentions of everyone involved, things don't work out the way you thought they would."

"As I am also not a fortune-teller, I fail to see how I can be held accountable for not fulfilling needs you did not voice to me. In addition to not being able to see the future, I cannot read your mind."

"Even if you could, I can only imagine that you would find it unworthy of listening to."

"When exactly did you become such a pain?" he asked, not bothering to temper his anger. "You were not like this before we were married."

"That's because before we were married, you paid me to be your assistant. An assistant is not a wife."

"I was very clear when I proposed to you that this would not be a typical marriage. That it would in fact reflect some of the duties that you took on as an assistant."

"Well, maybe nothing changed, then. Nothing

but me." She crossed her arms, closing herself off from conversation, and turned away from him.

He gritted his teeth, and determined that he would not speak to her again until they landed. Once they were on the island… He didn't know. But she wouldn't be able to escape him. Not until he allowed it.

If that was kidnapping, then so be it.

But he was not going to take the end of his marriage lying down. The sooner she realized that, the better.

CHAPTER FIVE

IT WAS STRANGE, landing on what you knew was your husband's private island, an island you had never been to before. He'd never brought her here, to this place, to this villa. It was incredible, like every property the Demetriou family owned. Just like the penthouse downtown that she was staying in while she avoided the reality of her life, just like the palace.

This was different. White walls, a red roof, placed on white sand in the middle of the blue, glittering bright sea. Like a beautiful piece of jewelry, perhaps part of the crown jewels. It was isolated, nothing like the palace, so filled with staff, tour groups and political leaders. Nothing like the penthouse, enveloped in the busy motion of the city.

She blinked against the sun, pale light washing over everything around them.

"Why don't you come in?"

She looked at Kairos, suddenly overcome by a sense of déjà vu. Of being in a new place with him, for the first time. That day she'd first walked into his office as his assistant.

"Come in. Sit down."

Tabitha shifted where she was standing, unable to decide what exactly she should be staring at. At the most beautiful, opulent surroundings she had ever seen, or at the most blindingly hand-some man she had ever laid eyes on.

She crossed the room, taking a seat across from him at his desk.

Tabitha was suddenly brought straight back into the present as she imagined that desk. The one they had conceived their baby on. Walking into his office that day, she never could have imagined that eight years later she would end up screwing him on it after asking him for a divorce.

She blinked against the stinging sensation in her eyes. They weren't tears. She was not going to cry any tears for him. For the man who didn't feel anything for her.

She followed him into the villa, unable to remain entirely unimpressed with her surroundings. She was used to opulence. She had spent years working with him in the palace prior to their marriage, and had had a good dose of exposure to it even before she herself was royalty. After nearly a decade in these kinds of settings she should be used to them.

But a small part of her was still very much that girl from the single-wide trailer, utterly unable to believe that she now rated entry into these sorts of places.

This—this small weakness for luxury—was the flaw in her armor. At least, the entry point by which to reach many of the others.

Everything in the room was white, large windows looking out over a lush garden, an infinity pool and beyond that the sea provided the only color. That was one of the first things she had noticed when she came to live in the palace. Even when she was simply in the apartments provided for her as an employee, the decor had been simple, but the quality unsurpassed.

It made her feel small and gauche to think of her observations now. The linens had been pure white, no pattern, or ornate embroidery to draw the eye. It was all in the feel of it. So soft it was like touching a cloud. Everything was like that. The tissues and the toilet paper even. Tiny pieces of luxury that added up to the kind of comfort she had never even imagined existed.

"My room is upstairs, at the end of the hall, feel free to choose whichever quarters suit you best."

She looked over at him, reminded yet again of that first meeting.

She had never seen an office quite like this. And she had never seen a man quite like him. When she entered the prestigious university that was currently facilitating this study-abroad program she'd been exposed to a higher class of people, a higher class of living than ever before. But this was somewhere far beyond that.

For one thing, he was a prince. No matter how blue the blood, that placed him several rungs higher on the social ladder than any of the old-money Americans she'd encountered. For another, he was unlike any of the other men she interacted with at university. He was a man, a real man, for a start, not a boy barely edging into his twenties.

In his perfectly cut custom suit he was daunting to say the least. Add the fact that his face was objectively the most beautiful masculine work of art she'd ever seen, and she found herself unable to speak. That never happened. She'd learned early on that if she wanted to improve her position in life she would have to attack her goals with single-mindedness. She could never afford to look like she didn't belong, because people would be all too willing to believe her. So she had cultivated confidence from the beginning.

It deserted her then. All her words drying up completely.

"It's nice to meet you," he said, not offering her his hand, but rather a simple incline of his head. "I have read your file, and taken the recommendation of my advisor into consideration.

However, I did not follow the advice. I merely took it under consideration."

She frowned, not entirely sure what to make of the comment. "Really?"

"Yes. A fact you should be grateful for, as he felt you were a bit too pretty to serve my needs."

Her face burned. But it wasn't with anger, as it should have been. Well, there was a bit of anger, but also a wave of excitement that had no business being there. "I was not aware my looks had anything to do with whether or not I would be a qualified assistant."

"They don't. Not to me. Though, I imagine his concerns center squarely around my younger brother, Andres, not me."

She was well educated on the royal family. Applying for a job at the palace without proper knowledge would be foolish. She was well familiar with Prince Andres and his reputation with women. She was also immune to such things. She was focused. She'd been accused of having tunnel vision by people who were nice, and of being frigid by people who weren't. None of it bothered her. She had goals. And once she reached those *goals she could expand her horizons. Until then, she would move on with a single-minded focus and make apologies to no one.*

No, Prince Andres didn't concern her.

The fact that some of her focus had splintered the moment she'd seen Prince Kairos concerned her a little bit. But that was an anomaly. Nothing to be concerned about. She would be back to normal as soon as she became accustomed to him, to the surroundings. Assuming she had a chance to do so.

"There's no need to be concerned," she said.

"You haven't met him yet."

"I don't need to meet him. I have not gotten as far as I have in my life by being silly, or easily seduced by princes. I'm here because this is not the kind of work experience that can be matched. I'm here because of what this will do for my résumé in the future. I'm not here to become the subject of tabloid gossip."

He smiled and the expression echoed in her stomach. "Then congratulations. I would like to hire you." And there he stood, extending his hand.

She stood as well, wrapping her fingers firmly

around his, ignoring the zip of heat that passed between them. She had just told him that she had no desire to become tabloid fodder, and she would not be undermined by betraying the fact that his touch affected her.

She buried it. Buried it down as deep as it would go.

"Excellent."

"Very. If you're ready, I can show you to your quarters."

"Do you need me to escort you?"

Tabitha blinked, coming back to the present sharply. "No. You can send my things up later. I'm assuming you had my things packed."

"No," he said. "However, your room should be stocked with all the amenities you might require."

"Translated into direct English, please, rather than your particular brand of doublespeak."

"I called ahead. Clothing, makeup and other toiletries should be delivered shortly. To the room of your choosing. There are no servants in residence at this house, that's part of the attraction to it."

"I wouldn't know, as this is the first time I've ever been here."

"I haven't been here since we were married, as you well know. I've been busy running the country."

"You're right. I am well aware."

She turned away from him then and walked up the stairs, acutely aware of his dark gaze following her every move. She didn't know why he should watch her with such attention now, when he had certainly never done so before.

She stiffened her posture and continued on, as though she were completely unaware of his attentions. She'd spent a very long time pretending she didn't notice how little he saw her. This should be no different.

She scoffed when she reached the landing and looked down the expansive corridor. There were a dozen rooms on this floor, at least. He had made it sound different somehow. Talking about his room being at the end of the hall, saying there were no servants in residence. Still, she should have known that his family owned nothing modest.

She selected the first door, if only because it would be the farthest away from him.

It was white like the rest of the rooms in the house. A four-poster bed was at the center, with gauzy, pale fabric draped over the carved wooden spires. The floor was marble with a plush rug at the center. The only color was provided by a jade vase positioned on a table set against the far wall, with bright cheery crimson flowers bursting from it. She wanted to take the vase, and the flowers, and hurl it to the ground.

Its very existence made her angry. As though it were trying to tell her she should be happy to be here. As though it were trying to prove that this was a wonderful, beautiful place.

Most of all, it made her furious because she had to wonder if this was the only room that contained flowers. If her husband had known she would choose this one because of its proximity, or lack thereof, to his room.

If he knew her so well, while not knowing her at all.

Suddenly, a wave of exhaustion washed over her. She was pregnant. Kairos had all but kidnapped her and brought her to an island. He wanted to negotiate, or terminate her parental rights.

She stumbled over to the plush bed, sinking down onto the covers. She felt weighted down by despair, as though her clothing were woven together with thread fashioned from lead. She closed her eyes, letting the bed pull her in as her clothing pushed her down. Her head was swimming with thoughts, confused, present and distant. Mainly, though, as she drifted off, she thought of Kairos. Of the day he asked her to be more than his assistant.

"Two weeks, Tabitha. The wedding was to be in two weeks' time. Now there is a video all over the internet of Francesca and Andres having my wedding night without me." Kairos's hands shook as he relayed the story, a glass of scotch in his hand, his normally completely cool demeanor fractured.

His dark hair was disheveled as though he had been running his hands through it, his tie loosened. She had so rarely seen her enigmatic boss

*appearing to be anything beyond perfectly com-
posed that Tabitha's resolve, built over the past
three years of working for him, was tested. And
was failing.*

*She had become accustomed to the taciturn
man who walked into his office in the morning,
barking orders, setting about the workday with
efficiency that was swift, brutal and beautiful to
behold.*

*This man, this man who seemed tested beyond
his limits, was a stranger to her. Brought her
right back to square one.*

"What are you going to do?" she asked.

*"You're my personal assistant, I thought you
might assist me."*

*She laughed, her stomach tightening. "Well,
cheating fiancées and doomed royal weddings
aren't really my forte."*

*"I thought everything was your forte," he said,
treating her to a look that burned her down to
her toes.*

*"After the wedding I'm leaving. You're going to
have another assistant. You're going to have to
get a little bit more self-sufficient." It was prob-*

ably the wrong time to bring that up, but she felt somewhat desolate about it. But she was done with university now, she had a business degree and had achieved most of it remotely while acting as Kairos's assistant, a special privilege given to her since she'd been selected for the job.

She should be excited. Looking forward to the change this would bring. To the advantage she would have with a degree from a prestigious school and three years of work experience for the royal family of Petras.

Instead, she felt as though she was being ripped away from her home. Felt as though she would be leaving a part of herself behind.

"I don't want another assistant," he said, his voice rough.

"That's just the alcohol and the emotional distress talking," she said.

"Perhaps. But nothing says that alcohol and emotional distress aren't honest."

"Probably more honest than the general state of things."

"Probably." He studied her hard. "I like you," he said, "I want you to know that."

Her stomach tightened further, her breath rushing from her lungs in a gust. "Well, that's flattering."

"You have been the perfect assistant, Tabitha. You have more poise than many women who were raised by kings. You are smart, diplomatic, and most importantly, you have not slept with my brother. Or, if you have, it wasn't captured on video."

She thought of the devastatingly handsome Prince Andres, and felt nothing. Kairos was the only man who had ever tested her resolve. And he never even tried. "I can honestly tell you that Andres has never so much as tempted me."

"Is there anything you do not excel at? Any skeletons in your closet?"

"I... You read my résumé."

"Yes. If you recall, I read yours and that of several hundred other hopefuls. You were indeed the most suitable. Beyond that which I could have ever anticipated." He set his glass of scotch down on his desk. "I don't know why I didn't see it before."

She couldn't breathe. God help her, she couldn't breathe. "See what?"

"Tabitha. I think you should marry me."

"Tabitha, are you well?"

Tabitha started at the sound of Kairos's voice. It was rare for her to be woken up by him. In fact, she couldn't recall if she ever had been. He didn't spend the night with her. He never had.

She opened her eyes, bright afternoon light filtering into her vision. She suddenly remembered where she was. Remembered that it was not that day when he first proposed, or any of the days in between that she'd spent as his wife. No, it was now. She was carrying his baby. They were divorcing.

The hopeful little ember that burned in her stomach, thanks to that dream, that memory, cooled.

"Not especially," she said, pushing into a sitting position and scrubbing her hands over her eyes.

Suddenly, she felt self-conscious, childish because of the gesture. She was not in the habit of waking up in front of him. For all that they had a physical relationship, they had very little intimacy.

She dropped her hands to her sides, balling them into fists.

"I brought your clothing up. And everything else."

"Did you…" She looked around the room. "Did you put it all away?"

"Yes. I was hardly going to ask you to do it. And as I said before, there are no servants in residence here."

"You don't have any service at all?"

"I occasionally employ the services of a chef. But for the purposes of this trip, some pre-prepared meals were brought along with your things."

"It's just you and me, then?"

He nodded, his dark gaze unreadable. "Yes."

"On the whole island?"

"On the whole island," he confirmed.

"Oh."

"What?"

"I don't think we've ever…really been alone before."

"We are very often alone," he said, frowning.

"In a palace filled with hundreds, in a building other people live in."

"I have never kidnapped you before either. You've also never been pregnant with my baby. Oh, yes, and we have never been on the brink of divorce. So, a season of firsts. How nice to add this to the list."

She stood up, stretching out her stiff muscles. "Where exactly do you get off being angry at me? We are here because of you."

"I'm angry with you because this divorce is happening at your demand."

"Had I not demanded we divorce, I wouldn't be pregnant."

"Had you not frozen me out of your bed perhaps you would have been pregnant a couple of months sooner."

She gritted her teeth, reckless heat pouring through her veins. "How dare you?" She advanced on him, and he wrapped his arm around her waist, pulling her close. "Don't."

Her protest was cut off by the press of his mouth against hers, hot and uncompromising, his tongue staking a claim as he took her deep, hard. She had no idea where these kinds of kisses had come from. Who this man was. This man who would spirit her away to a private island. Who kissed her like he was dying and her lips held his salvation.

It stood out in such sharp contrast to that kiss on their wedding night. The first time they had been alone in a bedroom like this. His kiss had been gentle then. Cool. She had waited for this moment. For heat to explode between them. Because she felt it. She had always felt it. It had been there from the moment she first walked into his office, no matter how hard she might try to deny it.

But everything he'd done had been so maddeningly measured, so unreasonably controlled. She had been shaking, from the inside out. With nerves, with desire. He had been gentle. Circumspect.

He left the lights off. That surprised her, because she had imagined that he would prefer to see her. At least, she had imagined that men preferred such things. She had no experience with them, and suddenly she regretted it. She hadn't. Never. Until now. Now, she was married to Kairos. She was his princess. She was his wife. And she had no idea how to please him.

They had two weeks to adjust to the idea of marrying each other, and during that two weeks he hadn't touched her. He had waited, because he'd said there was no point in doing anything differently. Not when it was so close. Not when he had the chance to do right by her.

She had told him, of course, that she was a virgin. In case he found the idea appalling in some way. In case he disliked the idea of being with a woman who had no practical experience. He had not been appalled. But it was then he'd insisted they wait.

So here she was, a bride dressed in white, and all that it symbolized, married to a man she didn't love. A man who did not love her, about to find out what all the fuss was about.

She might not love Kairos, but she was attracted to him. In her mind, this was ideal in many ways. She didn't love him. But she respected him. She cared for him. She was attracted to him. They had everything pleasant going for them, and nothing outrageous or unpleasant. Nothing that would turn them into the kinds of screaming monsters her parents had become under the influence of love and passion.

And so she waited. Waited for him to close the distance between them. But he was in no hurry. Finally, he crossed the room, a dark silhouette. She could see him working his tie, removing his jacket, his shirt. She could see nothing of his body, but she could tell that he was naked by the time he reached her. It was then that he kissed her. Cool, slow. Different to how she had imagined.

His skin was hot, but his movements were chilled and deliberate. He divested her of her gown quickly, making no ceremony of it. His touch was skilled, easily calling out a response in her as he teased her between her thighs, stroked his thumb over her nipples. But it was happening quickly, and she didn't know what she was supposed to do. Didn't understand her part in it. And he gave her no hints. He had her on her back quickly, testing her readiness with his fin-

gers. *Sliding one inside her first, then another, stretching her. He did this for a while, as though he were counting the time. As though he had read a textbook on how to make a woman's first time hurt as little as possible.*

Then he settled between her thighs and pushed into her quickly. She gritted her teeth against the pain, biting her lip to keep from digging her fingernails into his skin. She didn't have an orgasm.

He did. Of course he did.

He withdrew quickly after that, moving into the bathroom and starting a bath for her. Then he returned, ushering her in, waiting until she was submerged in the water before meeting her gaze. "I imagine you want some time alone."

No. She absolutely did not want time alone. She wanted him to hold her because she was pretty sure she was going to break apart. He had changed something deep inside of her. And he hadn't finished. She was shattered, but she wasn't remade.

"Yes," she heard herself saying, not sure where the response had come from.

"I'll see you in the morning."

* * *

She snapped back to the present, to this moment. To this kiss that bore no resemblance to anything that had occurred on that night. He had accused her of changing, but he wasn't the same either.

He kissed her neck, down to her collarbone, retracing that same path with the tip of his tongue. She found herself tearing at his shirt, her heart thundering hard, every fiber of her being desperate to have him. Desperate to have him inside her again. Like that night in his office. That night when the promise that had been broken on their wedding night was finally fulfilled.

I feel nothing.

His words from that night reached between them, hit her with the impact of a slap.

She pushed away from him, breathing hard. "Don't."

"You want to," he said, his words cutting and far too true.

"So? We don't have to do everything we want." She, of all people, truly shouldn't. "Anyway, I know from experience that sex with you produces a host of regrets."

"Do you regret being pregnant?"

"How can you not regret it? You're going to find a new wife." She disentangled herself from his hold, moving away from him, over to the window, turning her focus out to the view. Out to the sea below. "Having your heir belong to the wrong woman must be an upsetting prospect."

"Not especially. Because I do not intend to divorce you."

"Why?"

"You are having my child. There is no reason for me to marry another. None at all."

"So, you're suggesting we simply...*ignore* our marriage?"

"If you prefer. I should like to reach some kind of agreement with you, but you have been very unreasonable lately."

"And you have been a cold fish for the last five years."

She found herself being tugged back up against him, his lips crashing down on hers. He gripped her chin with his thumb and forefinger, his dark eyes blazing into hers. "Did that feel cold to you?" he ground out after they separated.

"You contrary man. Why do you only want something once it's been taken from you?"

He drew back as though she had slapped him. "I…"

"You can't deny it. And you don't have an answer."

His expression went blank. "If you regret the pregnancy, perhaps you should simply turn custody of the child over to me."

Everything inside of her screamed at the thought. "You misunderstand me," she bit out. "I don't regret having a child. I regret having *your* child. It would have been better for me to wait to get pregnant until I could find a man that I actually wanted to spend my life with."

He took a step back, his eyes filled with rage. His face, normally so controlled, normally schooled into such a careful, neutral expression, telegraphed every bit of his anger. "Such a pity then that it is my child you carry. Dinner is served in an hour. If you do not join me you can starve."

"Are you going to lock the kitchen?"

"I may yet. Do not test me, Tabitha, for you

will not like the result." He turned, walking out of the room, slamming the door hard behind him.

He had commanded that she not test him. And so that was exactly what she intended to do.

CHAPTER SIX

KAIROS COULD NOT fathom his own behavior. But then, he could not understand Tabitha's either. He had given her more credit than this. Had chosen her to be his wife because she was smart, faithful, levelheaded. Because she had served him as his assistant for years and never given him reason to distrust her. During his engagement to Francesca he had thought he might forge something of an emotional connection with her. His trust had been misplaced. Francesca had betrayed him with Andres.

He owed Andres a fair amount of anger for that. Both of them, really. And yet, he had never been able to muster much of it up. He was only grateful he had discovered Francesca's duplicity prior to making vows to her. And it had given him a chance to find someone better. To reevaluate what he expected out of marriage.

Women, it turned out, betrayed you eventually.
Well, you, specifically.

He took in a sharp breath, looking out through the living room at the terrace, at the table that was set with dinner for both of them. If she didn't come down…

He was seized with an image of himself storming back upstairs, flinging the door open, throwing her over his shoulder and carrying her down to the dinner table. Failing that, perhaps he would just throw her on the bed and finish what they had started earlier.

He gritted his teeth, battling against the erotic images that were battering against his mind's eye. Threatening to shatter his control. He had already behaved appallingly where she was concerned, and he would not compound his sins.

Why not? She left you. The one thing she promised she would not do.

He hated this. This feeling of helplessness. She inspired it in him more often than any other human being on the planet. From the first day they had married. He had never felt any hint of awkwardness around her when she was his PA.

And he'd been determined to hang on to that relationship. That meeting of the minds, the mutual understanding, that felt so right. It had made her the best assistant he'd ever had. By all rights, a nineteen-year-old from Middle America should never have been able to serve him the way that she had. And yet, for three years, she had been by far the most efficient and hard-working PA he'd ever had.

She'd transcended her circumstances and risen to the occasion. He imagined she would do that as a wife as well.

Though, it was disingenuous to pretend that all of the unforeseen issues fell on her shoulders. Their disastrous wedding night had been his fault.

He hadn't satisfied her. He had hurt her. And with his actions, it felt as though he had built a wall between them. Yes, a certain amount of distance was desirable. He didn't want to become emotionally entangled with her. Not with feelings that went beyond cordial affection.

But when they had entered her suite, and his

lips had touched hers for the first time without an audience, something had shifted inside of him. The rock wall he had built up around his control was cracking, crumbling. He had felt... a deep ache that had transcended anything he could remember feeling in recent years. A desire for something that he couldn't put a name to. Like seeing something familiar, shrouded in fog. Something that called to him, echoed inside of him, but that he couldn't identify.

Frustrating. Terrifying.

He went into the bathroom, running some hot water. She would probably be sore. He had done his best to make it as painless as possible, since he had known it was her first time, but he knew he had failed, on more than one level.

She didn't seem happy with him, when he ushered her into the bathroom.

He stood there, watching her as she submerged herself. It was a strange thing, seeing her naked now after so many years of looking at her as nothing more than an employee. Now she was exposed. Uncovered. He had been inside of her body...

He felt his own body stir in response to that memory. He had to go. Until he could get a handle on his response to her, he had to leave.

Unless she asked him to stay.

But he would not force that issue. Not after he had handled their first time so badly.

"I suppose you want some time alone?" he asked.

She shifted beneath the water, drawing her knees up to her chest and looking down. "Yes."

Her words rebuilt some of the wall inside of him. It was good. It reminded him of why distance was imperative. Why control mattered.

"I'll see you in the morning."

He walked out of the bathroom and dressed quickly in her room, before leaving and heading to his own quarters. Once he was inside, he stripped his clothing off again, heading straight for the shower. He turned the cold knob as far as it would go, stepping beneath the icy spray, gritting his teeth.

He would not repeat the same mistakes again.

He would not.

* * *

"I'm here." Tabitha's voice drew his attention to the top of the stairs. She was there, looking more beautiful than he could ever remember. Was this change happening inside of her beginning to affect her appearance? Her blond hair was loose, bouncing around her shoulders. So different to the usual restrained bun she often chose to wear.

Her dress was also completely unlike anything she would've worn back at the palace. But then, the instructions he'd left for the personal shopper tasked with amassing a small wardrobe for her here in the island hadn't been any more explicit than her size.

The dress had skinny straps and a deep V that made the whole gown appear to be resting precariously over her full breasts. It looked as if the slightest tug would snap those straps and see the dress falling down around her waist, settling on her voluptuous hips. She had applied a bare minimum of makeup, a light pink gloss to her lips, a bit of gold on her eyes. It was a more relaxed look than he was accustomed to seeing.

His body responded with a hunger that was becoming predictable.

"I'm glad you decided to join me."

"Well, now you won't need to put a lock on the pantry."

She began her descent, her delicate hand resting on the banister. His eyes were drawn to her fingers, to her long, elegant fingernails, painted a delicate coral that matched her dress.

"I'm pleased to hear that, *agape*."

"Don't call me that," she said, her tone sharp.

"What?"

"*Love*. It's always been a little bit of a farcical endearment, but it just stings all the more at the moment."

She breezed past him, heading outside to where the table was set for them. He followed after her, trying not to allow that helpless sensation to overtake him again. How did she do this to him? He ruled an entire nation. He was the master of his, and every domain, within its borders. Somehow she made him feel as inept as a schoolboy who didn't even have dominion over his own bedtime.

"I am sorry, I shall try to endeavor not to call you nice things," he said through clenched teeth.

She paused, looking over her shoulder, one pale eyebrow raised. "Just don't call me things you don't mean."

It was hard to think of a political response to that. Of course he didn't love her.

He cared for her, certainly. There was nothing duplicitous about his lack of emotion. He had made that clear when he proposed to her that afternoon in his office after his engagement to Francesca had blown all to hell. He had outlined exactly what the relationship between Tabitha and himself would be. Had told her he intended to base it upon the mutual respect they had for each other.

That thought, of just how honest he'd been, of how she had known fully, and agreed to this, re-ignited his anger.

And he forgot to search for the political response.

"Actually, my queen," he said, "I could instead call you exactly what you are. Not a queen. Simply a woman that I elevated far beyond her station. Far beyond what she was equipped to handle."

"Are you going to malign my blood now you've mixed your royal lineage with it? Perhaps you should have thought of that before you used my body as the vessel for your sacred heir."

She continued to walk ahead of him, her shoulders stiff. She took her place at the table, without waiting for him to come and hold her chair out for her. For some reason, the lack of ceremony annoyed him. Perhaps because it was yet more evidence of this transformation from his perfect, biddable wife, into this *creature*.

It wasn't perfect. And you know it.

He didn't like that thought. It only damaged the narrative he was constructing in his mind about the truth of his marriage. The one that absolved him from any wrongdoing.

The one that said he had told her how their marriage would work, and now she had an issue with it. That, the fact she had been warned, meant that now the fault rested on her alone.

It allowed him to open up all sorts of boxes inside of him, boxes he normally kept closed, locked tight, and pull out all the hurt and anger kept there, examining it, turning it over, holding it close to his chest.

He took his seat across from her, lifting his water to his lips. For a moment, he regretted not serving alcohol out of deference to her condition. She didn't deserve his deference.

"How is it you expected we might discuss things with more success cut off from civilization?"

"For a start," he said, leaning back in his chair, "I very much appreciate having you somewhat captive."

"I'm not sure how I'm supposed to feel about that."

"Oh, don't concern yourself. I'm not worried about how you feel."

"No, of course you aren't. Why start now?"

He set his water glass down hard enough that some of the clear liquid sloshed over the side. "I'm sorry, have I done something recently that conflicted with our initial marriage agreement?"

"You are…" She looked up, as though the clear

Mediterranean sky might have some answers. "You're distant. You're cold."

"A great many people might say that about you, *agape.*"

"Don't call me that," she said, blue eyes flashing.

"I don't recall agreeing to your edict, Tabitha."

"You want a list? I'm working on a list," she said, ignoring his words. "The only time in five years you ever bothered to get angry with me was when I told you I was going to leave you."

"You *want* me to get angry with you?"

"I want you to feel *something*. Anger would be a start."

"You have your wish. I am exceedingly angry with you."

"You barely speak to me. You only touch me when attempting to conceive. I am essentially part of the furniture to you. If you could have had an heir with a bureau in possession of childbearing hips, I've no doubt you would have done so."

"The same can be said of the way you treat me. Moreover, I never promised you anything different. What vow have I broken?"

A slash of color bled out over her pale cheekbones. "A woman expects her husband to treat her a certain way."

"Does she? Even when the husband told her exactly how things would be? If your expectations differ from the reality I lined out for you early on, I fail to see how that's my fault."

"Nobody imagines their marriage is going to be a frozen wasteland."

"A frozen wasteland is exactly what I promised you," he said, his tone biting. "If I had promised to love and cherish you, then I suppose you would have every right to feel cheated. To feel lied to. But I promised you respect, and I promised you fidelity, I promised that I would treat you as an equal. If I have failed on that score then it has only been in the days since you violated the promises *you* made to *me*."

"I know what you said. What *we* said, but... Five years on things feel different. Or they feel like they *should* be."

"I see. Were you ever going to tell me that? Or were you simply going to freeze me out until I was the one who asked for an end to the marriage?"

She curled her fingers into fists, and looked away from him. "That isn't…"

"Do you not enjoy being held accountable for the breakdown of our union, Tabitha? Because if I recall, you spent the past five years doing much the same thing you accuse me of. If an honest word has ever passed between us, I would be surprised. Did you think I didn't notice that you have grown increasingly distant? Did you think it didn't bother me?"

"Yes, Kairos, I imagined that it didn't bother you. Why would I ever assume that you cared about there being any closeness between us?"

"Because there was a time when I at least called you a friend."

Her golden brows shot upward. "Did you? Do you consider me a friend?"

"You know that I did. I assume you remember the day that I proposed to you."

"Oh, you mean the day that you watched a video of the woman you had chosen to marry having dirtier sex with your brother than I imagine you ever had with her? The day that you—drunkenly—told me you thought I would be a better choice to be your queen? I find it difficult to put much stock into anything you said that day."

"Then that's your mistake. Because I was sincere. I told you that we could build a stronger foundation than Francesca and I ever could. I told you that I had been having doubts about her even before her betrayal."

"Yes, that's right, you did. And why were you having doubts, exactly?"

"The way you behaved…it was such a stark contrast to Francesca, even on her best of days. I found myself wishing that it was you. When we traveled together, when I went to you to discuss affairs of the state…I found myself wishing that you were the one I was going to marry. I respected your opinion. And I felt like I could ask you questions, when with everyone else I had to simply know the answers."

He felt stripped bare saying these things now, without the buffer of alcohol, five years older and a lot more jaded than he had been then. But she needed to hear them. She needed to hear them again, clearly.

"And while it is a very nice sentiment, it isn't exactly the proposal every girl dreams of," she said, her tone brittle.

"It seems very much that you are angry with yourself for accepting a proposal you now deem beneath you. How high you have risen. That the proposal of a king is no longer good enough for you."

"Maybe I am the one who changed. But people do change."

"Only because they forget. You forget that you are going to have to leave my palace, leave Petras, search for a job. Struggle financially. Perhaps even face the life that you were so eager to leave behind. Marriage to me offered you instant elevation. The kind of status that you craved."

"Don't," she said, "you make me sound like I was nothing more than a gold digger."

"Oh, you would have done all right finding gold on your own. But validation? Status? For a piece of white trash from Nowhere, USA, that is a great deal more difficult to come by."

She stood, shoving her plate toward the center of the table. "I don't have to listen to you insulting me."

"You want me to call you something honest. Though, I hasten to remind you that I learned these words from you. This is what you think of yourself. You told me."

"Because I trusted you. Clearly, my own fault."

"No, I think I was the one who was foolish to trust you."

"We could go back and forth for days. But it doesn't solve anything. It doesn't erase the fact that I think we're better off apart. We should never have been a couple, Kairos, and you know it. As you said, I'm little more than a piece of white trash from a tiny town. You're the king of an entire nation. You wanted to marry someone else."

"You might be right. But it's too late for regrets. We are married to each other. And more than that, you're carrying my child."

"Plenty of people work out custody arrangements."

He stood, knocking his chair backward and

not caring when it hit the ground with a very loud thump. "And do those people still want each other? Do they exist constantly on the verge of tearing each other's clothes off and having each other on the nearest surface?"

The pink in her cheeks intensified. "You can only speak for yourself on that score."

"Really? I don't think that's true." He was suddenly gripped by lust, lust that mingled with the ever-present anger in his chest. He wasn't sure whether he wanted to yell at her, or press her against the wall and claim her body again. Both. He wanted both. Even though neither made sense. "You want me."

"Go to hell." They were the harshest words he'd ever heard on her lips. So much sweeter than the sophisticated chill had ever been.

"There. There at least, some honesty. Perhaps you should try it more often."

"I gave you honesty."

"Your version of honesty was a list of complaints that you could have, and should have voiced years ago. Ideally, before you accepted my proposal. What changed? What changed that you can no longer stand what you agreed would be enough to make a marriage?"

His words hit her with the force of the slap. And she just stood there, reeling. Tears prickled her eyes, her tongue was frozen. He was making too much sense. Making too good a case for how aggrieved he was by her request for divorce. He was right. She had not spoken an honest word to him. She hadn't asked him for what she wanted. Hadn't told him she was unhappy.

But she didn't know how to do it without opening herself up, and reviewing bits and pieces of pain that were best left hidden. Didn't know how to do it without confronting her fears. And anyway, she hadn't imagined that he would care.

She hadn't trusted herself enough to voice them. To deal with them.

She wasn't sure she trusted herself now.

"It isn't what I wanted," she said, her voice hollow.

"You just said what you wanted changed."

"Yes. No. It isn't that simple," she said, panic

gripping her neck, making it impossible for her to breathe.

"It seems fairly straightforward to me, *agape*, but then, I do not know much about the inner workings of the female mind. Throughout my life I have seen women act in ways that are inexplicable to me. My mother walking away from her position at the palace, Francesca compromising our union for a bit of stolen pleasure. You divorcing me. So, it comes as no surprise to me that I do not understand what you're trying to tell me now."

"You don't know everything about my past," she said.

It was for the best that he didn't. Best that he never did. She looked back on the Tabitha she'd been, before university, before she'd put distance between herself and her family, and saw a stranger.

But he didn't seem to know the Tabitha she was now. And she didn't know how to make him. Didn't know how to make him understand who she was. *Why* she was.

She didn't even know if it would change anything.

If nothing else, it would show him. Why he
should let her go. Why she wasn't suitable. And
it would remind her too.

"Do I not know you?"

"No. I know you did some cursory searching,
as far as I was concerned. My name. But you
don't know everything. In part because I don't
have the same last name as my mother, nor is her
name the same as the one listed on my birth cer-
tificate, not anymore. I don't share a name with
my stepfather either. Not having those names
excludes quite a lot from a cursory search. Of
course, you found nothing objectionable about
me. Nothing but good marks in school, no crim-
inal record, no scandal."

"Because that's all that mattered," he said,
something odd glittering in his black eyes.

"Yes. It is all that mattered. You were only
looking for what might cause problems with my
reputation, for you, as far as the public eye was
concerned. You weren't actually looking for anything real or meaningful about me."

"Come off your high horse, Tabitha. Obviously you didn't care whether or not I found anything meaningful out about you, because you deliberately concealed it from me."

She lifted her shoulder, her stomach sinking. "I can't argue with that. I can't argue with a great many of the accusations leveled at me today. I wasn't honest with you. I didn't tell you. I preferred to run away, rather than telling you what I wanted. But a lot of it is because… I don't actually know what I want. I started feeling dissatisfied with our relationship, and wanting more. And that confused me."

"Well, hell, if you're confused, what chance do I have?"

"I can't answer that question," she said, sounding defeated. Feeling defeated. "I don't know the answer. All I know is that I never thought I would marry. Then I met you, and I can't deny that I felt…attraction. It confused me. I had spent years getting through college, school of every kind, really, with a single-minded focus. I wanted to be better than my birth. I knew that education was the only way to accomplish that. I set about to get good grades, high test scores, so that I could earn scholarships. And I did that. I knew that if I split my focus, I wouldn't be able to. Then the internship at the palace came up, and I knew I had to seize it. I didn't have connections, I didn't have a pedigree. I knew that I needed a leg up in order to get the kind of job that I wanted."

"I imagine, ultimately, the chance to become queen of the nation was too great a temptation to pass up?"

She laughed, hardly able to process the surreal quality of it all even now. "I guess so. It was a lot of things. A chance to have you, physically, which I wanted. A chance to achieve a status that I'd never even imagined in my wildest dreams. I'm from nothing. Nothing and nowhere, and I wanted something more. And that… How could I refuse? Especially because your criteria suited mine so well. You see, Kairos, I didn't want love either. I didn't want passion."

"You said you were attracted to me."

"I was. I am. I suppose that's something I can't deny now. But I thought perhaps I could just touch the flames without being consumed by them. Then I realized that holding your fingertips over a blaze for five years is nothing more than a maddening exercise in torture. You're better off plunging yourself in or disengaging."

"And you chose to disengage?"

"Yes. I know that I can't afford to throw myself in."

"Why is that?"

"Reasons I haven't told you. Things you don't know."

"I'm not playing twenty questions with you, Tabitha, either tell me your secrets, or put them away. Pretend they don't matter as you did all those years. Jump into the fire, or back away."

Her throat tightened, her palms sweating. She hadn't thought about that day in years. She had turned it into a lesson, an object, a cautionary tale. But the images of the day, the way that it had smelled, the weather. The sounds her stepfather had made as he bled out on the floor, the screams of her mother when she realized what had been done… Those things she had blocked out. The entire incident had been carefully formed into a morality tale. Something that served to teach, but something she couldn't feel.

Not anymore.

Use what you need, discard the rest.

"I never wanted passion. Or love. Because…I shouldn't. I'm afraid of what I might be. What I might become. I think I've proven I have the capacity to act recklessly when I'm overtaken by strong emotion," she said, realizing that to him, the admission must seem ridiculous. For years all he had ever seen was the carefully cultivated cool reserve she had spent the better part of her teenage years crafting from blood and other people's consequences.

"Tell me," he said.

She was going to. Her heart was thundering in her ears, a sickening beat that echoed through her body, made her feel weak.

But maybe if she said it, he would understand. Maybe if she said it he would get why what he'd offered had seemed amazing. Why it had felt insufficient. Why she'd chosen to end it instead of asking for more.

"I was walking home from school. I was seventeen at the time. It was a beautiful day. And when I approached the trailer I could already hear them fighting. Not unusual. They fought all the time. My mother was screaming, which she always did. My stepfather was ignoring her. He was drunk, which he very often was."

She didn't let herself go back to that house. Not even in her mind. It was gritty and dirty and full of mold. But more than that. The air was heavy. The ghost of faded love lingering and oppressive, a malevolent spirit that choked the life out of everything it touched.

"I didn't know," Kairos said.

"I know," she said. "I didn't want you to." It stung her pride, to admit how low she'd started. To admit that she had no idea who her biological father was to a man for whom genetics was everything.

She was a bastard, having a royal baby. It seemed wrong somehow.

You always knew it would be this way. Why are you panicking now that it's too late?

Because the idea of it was one thing, the reality of it—all of it—her marriage, her past, her life, was different.

She'd spent the past year growing increasingly unhappy. And then Andres had married Zara. Watching the two of them physically hurt. It twisted her stomach to see the way they smiled at each other. Put a bitter, horrible taste in her mouth.

Made her feel a kind of heaviness she hadn't felt since she'd stood in that grimy little trailer.

"Tell me," he said, an order, because Kairos didn't know how to ask for things any other way.

"She kept screaming at him to listen. But he never did. She was so angry. She left the room. I thought she was going to pack, she did that a lot, even though she never left. Or that maybe she'd given up. Gone to take a nap. She did that sometimes too depending on how much she'd had to drink. But she came back. And she had a gun."

CHAPTER SEVEN

A COCKTAIL OF cold dread slithered down into Kairos's stomach. He could hardly credit the words that were coming out of his wife's mouth. Could hardly picture the gentle, sophisticated creature in front of him witnessing anything like this, much less being so tightly connected to it. Tabitha was strong. She possessed a backbone of steel, one he had witnessed on more than one occasion. When it came to handling foreign dignitaries, or members of the government and Petras, she was cool, calm and poised. When it came to organizing his schedule, and defending her position on hot-button issues, she never backed down.

But for all that she possessed that strength, there was something so smooth and fragile about her too. As though she were a porcelain doll, one that he was afraid to play with too roughly. For fear he might break her.

If she were that breakable, you would have shattered her on your desk.

Yes, that was true. He had not thought about her fertility then. Had not taken care with her, as he had always done in the past.

But still, he hadn't thought in that moment. He simply acted. This revelation challenged perceptions that he had never examined. Not deeply.

"What happened?" he asked, trying to keep his voice level.

"She shot him," Tabitha said, the words distant and matter-of-fact. Her expression stayed placid, as though she were discussing the contents of the menu for a dinner at the palace. "She was very sorry that she did it. Because he didn't get back up. He died. And she was sent to jail. I don't visit her."

She spoke the last item on the list as though it were the gravest sin of all. As though the worst thing of all was that she had distanced herself from her mother, not that her mother was a murderer.

"You *saw* all this," he said, that same shell he

had accused her of having wrapping itself around his own veins now, hardening them completely.

"Yes. It was a long time ago," she said, her voice sounding as if it was coming straight out of that distant past. "Eleven…twelve years ago now? I'm not sure."

"It doesn't matter how long ago it was, you still saw it."

"I don't like to think about it," she said, her blue eyes locking with his, looking at him for the first time since she had started telling her gruesome story. "I don't think you can blame me for that."

"No, not at all," he said.

"It wasn't relevant to our union. Not relevant to whether or not I would be good for the position."

"Except it clearly was, as I think it is probably related to the action you have taken now."

She looked down. "I can't argue with that. I was growing frustrated in our relationship, and I don't like to give those feelings any foothold on my life. I don't like to allow them free rein."

"Surely you don't think you're going to find a gun and shoot me?"

"I'm sure my mother didn't think she would

do that either," Tabitha said, starting to pace, her hands clasped in front of her. She was picking at the polish on her fingernails, something he had never seen her do before. It was then he noticed that she wasn't wearing her ring. How had he missed it before?

Perhaps you were too wrapped up in imagining those fingers wrapped around your member to notice.

He gritted his teeth. Yes, that was the problem. Whatever had exploded between them was stealing his ability to think clearly.

"Where is your ring?"

She stopped thinking and looked at her fingernails. "I took it off."

"It was very expensive," he said, though that was not his concern at all, and he wasn't sure why he was pretending that it was.

"I know. But it is also mine. That was part of our prenuptial agreement if you recall."

"I don't need the money, I was just concerned something might have happened to it."

"It's in a safe. In a bank. It's fine. But there is

no point in me wearing it when I'm not your wife. I would hate to start gossip in the press."

"We already have."

"Imagine the gossip if they knew my past as well."

"Enough. No one is going to find out. Because I will not tell. Anyway, it is not a reflection on you."

"Isn't it? My genetics. Our child's genetics."

"If blood determined everything I would be a tyrant or absent." He didn't like to speak of his parents. Talking about his father, and his rages, was much simpler than talking about his mother, who was not there at all. But either way, it was a topic he preferred not to broach.

"Well, you're neither of those things," she said, "but Andres isn't exactly well-adjusted."

Kairos laughed, thinking of his brother and the large swath of destruction Andres had spent the first thirty years of his life cutting through the kingdom, through Kairos's own life. "He has settled, don't you think?"

Tabitha laughed. "I suppose he has. I'm not quite sure how they managed. A real marriage. Especially out of their circumstances. If any marriage came about in a stranger way than ours, it's theirs."

"Zara is not exactly conventional. Or suitable," Kairos said.

Tabitha looked up at him, deep, fathomless emotion radiating from her blue eyes. "Perhaps I should have been more unsuitable?"

Her words made his heart twist, made his stomach tighten. "Tabitha, I cannot imagine the things you have seen," he said. He wasn't sure why he said it. But then, he didn't know what else to say.

"I'm the same person."

The same person from before she had told him about her experience, he knew that was what she meant. But for him it only highlighted the fact that he didn't truly know her at all. She was right. The Tabitha who had witnessed the murder of her stepfather was the same woman he had been married to for the past five years. The same woman he had known for nearly a decade.

But he didn't *know* her. Not really. How could he? She was all things soft, beautiful and contained, and he had imagined she had grown that way, like a plant that had only ever experienced life in a hothouse.

It turned out she had been forged in the elements. An orchid put to the test in a blizzard. And she had come out of it alive. Beautiful. Seemingly untouched.

It humbled him in a strange way.

"We do not know each other," he said.

"I've been saying that," she said.

"Yes, you have been. But I didn't realize how true it was until now. You know *my* life, so I did not imagine there were such secrets between us."

"We don't talk about your life," she said, "not beyond what you had for dinner last night."

He couldn't argue with the truth of that statement. "There is nothing to tell. The evidence of my life is before you. You have seen who I am by my actions. I don't see the point in rehashing how I felt when my mother left."

"You felt something," she said, her voice muted.

"Of course I did," he said. The very thought opened up a pit of despair inside of him. Helplessness. And a dark, black rage he would rather not acknowledge lived within him. "We are strangers."

"Strangers who have sex," Tabitha added.

"Yes," he said, "certainly. And yet, I'm not even entirely certain I know your body."

Her cheeks turned pink. "You did all right with it last month."

"And the times before that?" This line of questioning was not pleasant for him. What man liked calling his own prowess into question? But it wasn't so simple as prowess. He had the ability, but he'd always held back with her. Always.

That was the very beginning of where he had gone wrong. He had imagined that he needed to go slowly, that he needed to mitigate the passion between them.

The truth of it was he had been attracted to her from the moment she walked into his office. Even during his engagement to Francesca. And while he had never acted on it, it had been there, shimmering beneath the surface like waves of heat over the sand. He wanted her. He had always wanted her.

He had kept a part of himself closed off because it was so strong. Because, like her, he rejected strong emotion, strong desire.

But perhaps it would be possible to open up the physical, to have that, while keeping the rest of it safe. Perhaps it might give her what she craved. Or at the very least thaw some of the chill that was between them.

"Yes, I did then. Or, maybe my clumsiness was simply covered by the explosion between us," he said.

"There was nothing clumsy about it," she said, the color in her cheeks intensifying.

"I have held back every time we've been together," he said. "Except then."

"Why have you held back?"

"Why have you?"

"I think I explained that." She swallowed visibly. "Anyway, it doesn't matter. We don't work. We've established that."

"Have we?" Desperation clawed at him like a wild beast. "I'm not sure that's true. We've both admitted to holding back. And I think it's safe to say that we're both liars."

"I never lied to you."

"There is one very specific word I can think of

in response to that. It has to do with the excrement of a bull."

"Crassness does not suit you, Kairos."

"Or, perhaps it does," he said. "How would you know?"

"I wouldn't. And it isn't my job to know. The function of ex-wives is just to walk off into the distance and spend all of your money. It isn't to know you."

"All right," he said, an idea pushing its way into the forefront of his mind even as the words exited his mouth. "You will be free to do so. But I have conditions."

She frowned. "What are you talking about? We both know I don't actually get any of your money."

"It doesn't have to be that way. The prenuptial agreement is very rigid. And I am a man of means. It is unreasonable of me to withhold a portion of that from you after all you have…suffered at my hands. Moreover, you are the mother of my child and therefore a consistent lifestyle will need to be kept whichever household he is staying in at a given time, don't you agree?"

"I don't…I don't understand."

"As I said, there will be conditions to this agreement."

"What do you want?"

What he wanted was for everything to go back as it had been. What he wanted was the wife she had been all those years ago. The wife he had imagined she would be forever. The perfect complement to the man he presented to her, the man he presented to the world. Yes, they were liars, but they had told such compatible lies. Such quiet lies.

This explosion of truth wasn't compatible, and it wasn't quiet. It had left rubble and shrapnel everywhere, the shattered pieces of the life they once had littering the ground in front of them. There was no ignoring it. There would be no putting it back together as it was. But he wouldn't leave it. Wouldn't give up.

They were having a child together. He would not be an absentee father. He would not allow her to be a distant mother. There would be no echoes of his childhood. Not if he had anything to do about it.

And he *did*. He was king, after all.

"Two weeks. I want fourteen days of honesty. I want your body, I want your secrets. I want everything. And if, at the end of that time, you feel like you still don't know me, if then, you feel like you cannot make a life with me, then I will give you your divorce. And with it, much more favorable terms than we originally agreed upon. Money. Housing. Shared custody."

"Why?" She looked stricken, as though he had told her she had to spend two weeks in the dungeon, rather than two weeks with her husband.

"It doesn't matter why. I am your king, and I have commanded it. Now," he took a deep breath, trying to cool the flame that was roaring through his veins. One of triumph. One of arousal. "Either take off your dress, or tell me another secret."

CHAPTER EIGHT

TABITHA'S HEART WAS pounding so hard, she thought she might pass out. She wasn't entirely certain whether she was living in a nightmare, or a fantasy. Kairos did not ask her to take her clothes off. He just didn't. He didn't make demands of her like this at all. And yet, there was no denying that now, her normally cool and controlled husband was looking at her with molten fire in his dark eyes, his gaze intense, uncompromising.

"I'm certain that you did not command me to take my dress off here on the balcony." Retreating into her icy facade was the most comfortable response she could find. After all, the cold didn't bother her. It was this heat, this searing, uncompromising heat that arched between them.

"I am certain that I did." The sun had lowered in the sky some since they had first come outside, and now the rays cut through the palm trees, illuminating his face, throwing his high cheekbones and strong jaw into sharp relief. He looked like a stranger. Not at all like the man she had married. A man who would never have made such a command of her. She was shaking. Shaking from the inside out. Because she had no choice. Had no choice but to accept his devil's bargain. She would be a fool not to. He was offering her a chance to raise her child without struggle, without fighting for custody, without fighting for the bare necessities.

But deeper than that, more shamefully than that, she simply wanted to obey. Even though she could hardly imagine it. Slipping her dress off her body, out here, in the open air, the breeze blowing over her skin. To just let go of everything. Of her control. Of her fear.

"We're the only ones here." His words jolted her out of her fantasy.

He was right, of course, there was no one else here. There was no one to see. But that wasn't what concerned her. The fact that there was no one around only frightened her more. There would be no consequences here. No one to stop them. No perfectly planned and well-ordered events on their calendar to interrupt. No rules, no society, no sense of propriety. There was nothing to stop her from stripping off her clothes, from closing the space between them and wrapping herself around his body, giving herself over to this desperate, gnawing ache that had taken her over completely.

She turned away from him, heading toward the entrance to the villa. She felt the firm hand on her shoulder, and found herself being turned around, pressed against the wall. Her eyes clashed with his, electricity skittering along her veins, collecting in her stomach. "Where do you think you're going?"

"Away from you. Away from here. Because you're crazy."

"Your king gave you an order," he said, his tone shot through with steel. It should make her angry. It should not make her feel restless. Shouldn't make her breasts ache. Shouldn't make her feel slick and ready between her thighs. But he did. *He* did.

His anger, his arrogance—never directed at her before, not like this—was a fresh and heady drug she'd never tried before.

"I see." She swallowed hard. "And will he punish me if I don't comply?"

"I would have to set an example," he said, his tone soft, steady and no less strong.

"For who? As you have already stated, there is no one here."

"For you. For the future. I cannot have you thinking you can simply defy me. Not if this is to work."

"I haven't agreed to—"

He reached up, gripped her chin and held her tight. "You may not have agreed to stay with me forever, *agape*. But you have no choice other than to agree to this two weeks. I do not wish to spend any of that time arguing with you. Not when I could find other uses for your mouth."

She gasped, pressing herself more firmly against the wall, away from him. Erotic images assaulted her mind's eye. Of herself, kneeling before him. Tasting him, taking him into her mouth.

She had never done that before. Not with him, not with anyone.

Strange, now she thought about it. Other people traded that particular sex act so casually, and she had never even shared it with her husband.

It didn't disgust her. To the contrary, it intrigued her. Aroused her. And yet, she was shrinking away from him as though she were afraid. She would not be so easily cowed. Would not allow him to claim total control in this way. She was strong. She had not got to where she was in life by folding in on herself. He might be the king, but she was a queen, for God's sake.

"Could you? That would be a first, then." She lifted her hand, curved it around his neck, losing her fingers through his hair. "Shall I get on my knees and bow down before Your Majesty?"

It was his turn to draw back, dark colors slashing his high, well-defined cheekbones. "I did not mean…"

Of course he didn't. He never meant such salacious things. Ever. He had likely only been thinking of a kiss. He probably hadn't even intended for her to take her dress off.

On the heels of that thought, her hand moved to her shoulder and flicked the strap of her dress down. "Words are powerful," she said, pushing at the other strap so they both hung down. "Once they're spoken you can't erase them. Even if you didn't intend for them to be taken in a certain way. Once you speak them, they belong to whoever hears them." She reached behind her back, grabbing a hold of the zipper tab and drawing it down to the middle of her back. The top of her dress fell, exposing her bare breasts to him.

"Tabitha," he growled, his tone a warning.

"What is it? Is my obedience not to your liking? Is this yet another one of our miscommunications?" She pushed the dress down her hips, taking her panties with it, standing before him, naked, and, somehow, not embarrassed.

"You seemed so confident this was what you wanted only a moment ago."

He said nothing as she lowered herself to the patio in front of him. She was shaking. And she wasn't entirely certain if it was the desire or rage. Or if it was some twisted, unholy offspring of the two, taking her over completely. She wasn't entirely certain it mattered. Just as she was sure in-experience wouldn't matter here either. She didn't know what sorts of things Kairos had done with women before her. They barely talked about their own sex life, so they'd had no reason at all to dis-cuss experiences either of them had had prior to their marriage. Of course, for her, there hadn't been so much as a kiss. As far as he went? He was a mystery to her.

But one thing she knew for certain, if he was as faithful to her as he claimed to be, no one had done this for him in at least five years. Time healed all wounds, and likely erased memories of oral pleasure. At least, she could hope.

She reached up and grabbed hold of his belt buckle, working the leather through the metal clasp. Her hands were shaking, as much from nerves and determination as from desire. It was impossible for her to tell if this was really her de-fining move in a power play, or if she was sim-ply acting out of need. Out of lust. She supposed that didn't matter either.

He reached down, grabbing a fistful of her hair,

stopping her short. "Tabitha. I would not ask this of you."

She looked up at him, at the desperation in his dark eyes, and something twisted, low and painful inside of her. "Why do you think it's a sacrifice?"

"It offers nothing to you."

"Isn't that what this two weeks is about? My service to you?" She immediately regretted the words the moment they left her mouth. That it was too late to call them back. As she had only just said to him, once words were spoken they could not be erased.

"No," he said, his voice rough, "I do not require you to lower yourself in this way."

Her eyes stung, a deep, painful ache that started behind them and worked its way forward. She said nothing. Instead, she tugged his pants and underwear down slightly, exposing his rampant masculinity to her. She didn't often examine his body. More often than not, they made love in the dark. If she ever saw him naked, it was most likely an accident.

Her breath hissed through her teeth as she

ran her palm over his hardened length. He was beautiful. Five years, and she had never had the chance to truly appreciate that. Five years and she had never knelt before him in this way, had never even contemplated doing what she was about to do. She had been so determined to keep control, so absolutely hell-bent on maintaining the facade of the perfect ice queen that she'd even allowed her fantasies to become frozen.

She regretted it now, bitterly. Wasted time freezing in the cold when she could have been warm. Like sleeping out in a snowbank only to discover that the front door had been unlocked the whole time, the lit hearth in a warm bed available to her if she had only tried.

Why had she never tried?

She curled her fingers around him, leaning forward and flicking the tip of her tongue out across his heated flesh. His hips flexed forward, a harsh groan escaping his lips. His fist tightened on her hair, so tight it hurt. Yet, she didn't want him to release her. Didn't want him to pull away.

He didn't. And so she kept on. Exploring the entire length of him slowly, relishing the flavor of him. She raised her eyes and met his as she shifted, taking him completely into her mouth.

"Tabitha," he said, his tone warning even as he tugged her head back sharply.

She resisted him, not allowing his hold to interrupt her exploration, tears pricking her eyes as he pulled hard on her hair. It occurred to her then how debauched the whole scene must look. How very unlike her and Kairos it was. Her naked, at his feet, with him mostly dressed, standing out there on the terrace of his fine, well-ordered home, the gentle beauty of the ocean acting as a backdrop to their licentious activities.

That thought only aroused her further. She had no confusion about what she felt now. None at all.

She was starving. Starving for a banquet that had been laid out before her for five long years while she wasted away in an abstinent state. And she was going to have her fill.

She rested her hands on his thighs, could feel his muscle shaking beneath her palms. Could feel just how rigorously she tested his control. She was drunk on the power of it, drunk on him. On a desire that she had kept buried so deep, so well hidden, even she might have been convinced that it wasn't there.

But now that she had brought it out, opened the lid, set it free, she was consumed by it.

She didn't know this creature. This creature down on her knees, uncaring that the cement bit into her skin, unconcerned with the fact that she was naked, outside, with the sun shining on her bare skin. She was not, in this moment, the sophisticated woman she had fashioned herself into in order to walk freely in Kairos's world. But she wasn't the girl from the trailer park either. She was something new, something wholly and completely different. And in that was a freedom she had not anticipated.

She had not moved from one cage into another, as she had imagined she might. Rather, she had slipped through the bars completely.

Suddenly, she found herself being hauled to her feet. "Not like this," he said, his tone dark and rough. "I need to have you properly."

She expected him to release his hold on her, to allow her to go back into the house and walk up the stairs, so that they might find a bed or some other civilized surface to complete their exceedingly uncivilized activities.

But as much as she had surprised herself in the past few minutes, Kairos surprised her even further. He turned toward the table, sweeping his hand across the high-gloss surface and sweeping their plates onto the ground, the porcelain shattering, the silver clattering on the hard surface.

Then she found herself being laid down on the pristine white tablecloth, his large body covering hers as he tested her readiness with the blunt head of his erection. He bent his head, kissing her neck, blazing a trail down to her breasts, sucking one nipple deep into his mouth as he sank into her body.

He filled her so completely, so utterly. She shuddered with the pleasure of it. This act had become so painful in the past couple of years. So intimate, the act of two bodies becoming one, and yet a brick wall might as well have existed between them even while they lay as close as two people possibly could.

But that wasn't happening now. Now, she felt him go so deep she was certain he touched her heart. There was no darkness to shield her body from his gaze, none to protect her from the look in his eyes. So she met them, boldly, even though she knew she was taking a chance on finding no connection there. On seeing nothing but emptiness.

They weren't empty. They were full. Full of heat, fire and a ragged emotion she could think of no name for.

It didn't matter, because soon she couldn't think at all. She was carried away on a tide of pleasure, molten waves wrapping themselves around her body until she was certain she would be consumed completely, dragged to the bottom never to resurface.

Just when she thought she would burst, when she was certain she couldn't endure another moment, pleasure exploded deep inside of her, rippling outward. She held on to him tightly, counting on him to anchor her to earth. Then he began to shake, his movements becoming erratic as he gave himself up to his own release.

She turned her head to the side, looking down at the ground, puzzled by the spray of glass she saw. And then it all slowly came back to her, piece by piece. They were on the table. He had broken the plates. The glasses. Had left the food strewn all over the ground for the birds.

He had been…he had been consumed by desire for her.

It was only then she realized that the table surface was uncomfortable. And even with that realization she didn't want to move. Because he was still inside of her, his chest pressed against hers. And she could feel his heart beating. Could feel just how affected he had been by what had passed between them. Could see the evidence all over the ground.

"What happens if we get hungry later?" The question fell from her lips without her permission. But she hadn't eaten very much of her dinner, and it seemed an important thing to know.

"There is plenty in the pantry. There are biscuits."

"American or European?"

"European," he said.

It seemed a little bit absurd to be discussing cookies in such a position.

She was about to say as much when she found herself being swept up into his arms again. She expected to be set on the ground, but he kept her scooped up, held tightly against his chest. "You don't have shoes," he said. She looked down, and saw that he was still wearing his. He stepped confidently over the remains of their plates, shards of glass cracking beneath each of his steps. He brought them both into the house, continuing through the living room and up the stairs. "There will be no question of you sleeping alone."

"We never share a room," she said.

Never. Not from the first moment. The first heartbreaking night of their marriage when he had left her sitting alone, having just lost her virginity with nothing more than a warm bath for comfort.

"We only have two weeks, *agape*," he said, not heeding her request that he refrain from endearments, "and if two weeks is all there is, then I will take every moment."

For the second time in the space of less than twenty-four hours, Kairos watched Tabitha sleep. He found it fascinating. Yet another facet to his wife he hadn't seen over the course of the past few years. Surely she must've dozed off on flights, long car rides. She *must* have.

But he couldn't picture it. The only image he had in his head was that of Tabitha sitting with rigid posture, her hands folded in her lap. Did he truly take so little notice of her? Or was she simply so uncomfortable in his presence that she couldn't do anything but sit as though her life depended on her balancing a book on her head.

She was thoroughly exhausted now. From what had transpired downstairs during dinner.

Erotic images flashed before his mind's eye. Of her kneeling before him. Of him begging her not to.

It was an act he simply wasn't comfortable with. He didn't want someone serving him in that way. Giving him pleasure while he recipro-cated nothing. And yet, the moment her tongue had touched him he had been lost. He had not been holding her hair to move her away from him, but rather to anchor himself to the ground.

He was lying next to her now, still naked, but

not touching her. She was sleeping on her side, her elbow beneath her cheek, her knees drawn up slightly. She looked young. Vulnerable. Everything she was. Though she wore the facade of a stone wall, he knew she was soft beneath it. He just chose to ignore it when it suited him.

She stirred, rolling onto her back, stretching her arms up over her head, her breasts rising with the motion.

Kairos had never been one to gaze at art. He found it a pointless exercise. The world had enough to offer in terms of beauty without adding needless glitter to it. But she was art, there was no other word for it. She looked as though she was perfectly formed from marble, warm life breathed into her making her human, but still almost impossible in her loveliness. And he was turning into a fool, thinking in poetry, which was something he held in even lower esteem than art.

Her blue eyes opened slowly, confusion drifting through her expression. "Kairos?"

"Yes. Two weeks. The table."

She blinked. "Oh. Yes. That happened."

"Yes."

"I'm hungry," she said, pushing herself into a sitting position, causing her breasts to move in yet more interesting ways.

"I think I can help with that."

CHAPTER NINE

TABITHA WAS BAREFOOT, wearing nothing but Kairos's white dress shirt, the crisp fabric skimming the tops of her thighs. She was certain that her makeup had come off sometime between dinner, being ravished on the table and sleeping for at least three hours afterward.

She didn't make it a habit of being so uncovered in front of him. He never saw her with messy hair, or mascara streaked down her cheeks. And she never saw him as he was now. Shirtless, wearing nothing but a pair of black dress pants. His feet were bare too, and she found something strangely erotic about it.

This was the sort of thing she imagined most couples would take for granted after five years. Rummaging around for food late at night, barely dressed after an evening of sex on the dinner table.

Well, she imagined that sex on the dinner table wasn't all that typical regardless of the type of relationship you had.

The memories made her face heat, made her body feel restless.

She didn't know who she was. Not anymore. The thought should scare her, because she'd left normalcy and control, the things she had prized for so many years, shattered on the floor of the balcony.

But she was going to eat cookies with Kairos, after just getting a taste of the man she'd always suspected lurked somewhere beneath the starched shirts and perfectly straight ties.

It was hard to care about anything else.

"You promised cookies," she said, backing against the kitchen counter, folding her hands in front of her reflexively. It was the position she often assumed around Kairos. It kept her posture straight, kept her from reaching out and touching him, or anything silly like that. It was more of a concern right now than it usually was.

It seemed silly. She should be satisfied, at least marginally. That was hands down the best sex they'd ever had. And what had happened between them a month ago had been pretty amazing. Still, this had nearly obliterated the memory of that.

Forget all the years that had come before it.

"I did," he said, turning toward one of the cabinets and opening it.

She watched much closer than necessary as he reached up to grab a tin that was placed on the top shelf. The muscles in his back bunched and shifted as he moved. She felt a strange, reckless sensation wind its way through her body. Like a shot of adrenaline straight to the system.

"The cookies," he said, turning to face her, the Americanized term sounding strange on his lips. "As promised. Because *I* keep my promises."

"Do you intend to badger me constantly?" she asked, reaching out and taking the tin from his hands. "Make sure I keenly feel the depths of the wound left in you by my betrayal?"

"If badgering is what it takes," he said, "then certainly."

"I promised you two weeks. I don't see the point in you haranguing me constantly." She pried the lid off the tin and reached inside, pulling out a piece of shortbread and lifting it to her lips. She nibbled on it slowly, watching his expression to see if she might find any clues to what he was thinking. As usual, there were none.

"I'm not haranguing you," he said. "I'm simply a man who knows what he wants."

"Yes, you want me to keep on being your wife. For your continued convenience."

"Yes, for my continued convenience. For the welfare of our child as well, if you have forgotten."

Her stomach sank. The truth was, for a moment, she *had* forgotten. It was so easy to forget about the tiny life she carried inside her womb. After all, she had found out less than twenty-four hours ago. And in the time since then she had been extradited to a private island by her estranged husband, made love to enthusiastically on a table and had eaten cookies barefoot in a kitchen. All of it was a bit out of the ordinary.

It was difficult for her brain to decide which particular extraordinary detail to hold on to. She had a feeling it was protecting her from reality a bit, too. Preserving her from the stark truth that she was going to bring a child into a very unsettled situation.

"Of course I haven't forgotten," she said, because the alternative would most certainly break the spell that was momentarily cast over him. He would take a dim view to her forgetting that she was carrying his baby. The baby was the only reason he was attempting reconciliation with her, after all.

"Honesty, Tabitha," he said, his tone chastising, "we have an agreement that we will strive for honesty over this two weeks."

"Sex is easier," she returned, ignoring the heat that assaulted her cheeks. "And more fun."

A strange expression passed over his face. "You have no argument from me on that score."

"Cars," she said, looking at his handsome face, trying to do something to get a handle on the heat that was still thrumming through her veins.

"What about them?" he asked.

"Why do you like them? It's strange. You're a very practical man. Cars don't seem especially practical."

"I don't suppose they are," he said, leaning

back against the counter, curling his fingers over the edge and gripping it tight. "But I…I never had hobbies. While my peers were out going to parties and…whatever else they did, I was studying. Not just to get through school, and then university, but studying everything my father did so that I could emulate him. I didn't deviate from his lesson plan for my life. One of the very few normal things I learned was how to drive. It was a practical skill, after all, so he allowed one of his men to teach me. I learned quickly and…for me, that was my only bit of freedom. I would take drives across the country. Alone. Otherwise I was never alone. There was always security detail, or my father or one of his advisors. So that's why I like cars. Freedom and solitude."

She swallowed hard, an unexpected lump of emotion lodging itself in the center of her chest. She hadn't expected anything so complete. So honest. "Your father didn't teach you himself?"

"No," he said. "He was very busy."

She nodded. "Of course."

She hadn't known the king well. By the time they'd married, the old man's health was declining and he hadn't had the energy to take many visitors, much less a commoner daughter-in-law put into place because of his disappointing younger son's scandalous behavior.

"I didn't want him to teach me anyway," he said.

"Why not?" she asked.

"Because I loved it. My father had a way of taking things I loved and turning them into something forbidden. Something I couldn't have." A muscle in his jaw ticked. "I didn't want him to do that with the cars."

"What did he do?"

"He was so very concerned about forming me into the kind of leader Petras needed. A man of principles. A man of control. Levelheaded. When I…when I showed too much enthusiasm, he was eager to snuff it out."

"Why?" she asked, her heart twisting for him.

"Because. He knew that distractions could become weaknesses. Easily."

He pushed away from the counter, closing the space between them, close enough she could feel the heat from his body. Far enough that she couldn't quite touch him. But oh, how she wanted to. How she craved this man.

It wasn't a new hunger, but it was reinvigorated. The tastes of him she'd had made her crave him all the more. Where before, she could control it... now it felt somewhere beyond her.

"Was it there the whole time?" he asked, his voice rough.

Her heart slammed into her chest and she looked down at her hands, frowning deeply when she noticed a large chip in her polish. Strange. She'd just painted them. "Was *what* there?"

"This. This insanity. Was it in you? In me? Was it between us from the very start, needing only a bit of anger to act as an accelerant?"

She lifted her shoulder. "I don't know."

Except she had a feeling she did. It was in her. She knew it. Perhaps it was in both of them. Which made them a deadly combination if ever there was one.

All it took was a little bit of anger. All it took was a little bit of anger to ignite a spark and start a blaze. But whether or not that blaze would be contained to last, or whether he would turn to violence, she didn't know.

She pressed the edge of her thumbnail against the polish on her ring finger and stripped a large flake of coral away.

She blinked, quickly realizing she'd been responsible for the other chip as well. Something she'd always done to her manicures when she was younger. Something she'd trained away.

She was regressing.

"It has never been like this for me. Not with any other woman. I have never…" A crease appeared between his dark brows. "I have never allowed a woman to do for me what you did out on the terrace."

"Oral sex?" she asked, her brows raised. She was a little bit embarrassed by her own frankness, but she hadn't been able to hold it back. Anyway, what was the point of being embarrassed to say something when you had already done it? It didn't make much sense.

"Yes," he said through clenched teeth. "It is not something I ever saw much use in."

"The way I hear tell of it, most men find it extremely useful."

"Have you done that before? For other men?" There was an edge to his voice now. Jealousy. That Kairos could be jealous over who had received her favors made her feel reluctantly satisfied.

She looked up at him, her heart thundering. "If I had?"

"I would call him a lucky bastard. And I would *probably* not put a price on his head."

"That's quite proprietary of you, Kairos," she said. "Very out of character."

"Have I been *in* character for any moment in the past month, Tabitha? Answer me that."

"Not in your character as I know it," she answered carefully.

"Not as I know it either. Staying in control is usually so much easier."

"I test your control?"

"Do you not see?"

"I haven't—" she took another bite of her cookie "—not for five years."

"I suppose I became much more desperate

when I thought I might lose you. I could feel this," he said, the admission raw, "this thing between us. I realize now that I could always sense it there."

His words echoed with truth, reflecting everything she knew down deep inside.

"But I never wanted… It is not what I wanted for my marriage," he continued. "My parents were never happy. My father was distant, a man who put his country before all else, because what is a king but a servant to his people? He was not a loving father. He was not warm. He could be very hard. Especially on Andres. But I considered what he gave to me to be guidance. Necessary. He knew that I would someday be as he. A king. But he was not married to you. He was married to a temperamental, flighty woman who let every bump in the road upset her. Who felt things too deeply. I vowed that I would find a woman who was different. You were perfect. Such perfect reserve. And then, the first time I ever touched you, the first time we made love, there was something else there. The very thing I didn't want. That kind of uncontrollable desire that leads to poor decisions made in anger and desperation."

"I didn't want that either," she said, her voice soft.

"I know you didn't want it. Now you resent me for making sure that I did what we both claimed we needed in a marriage? For keeping you at a distance when you asked for that distance?"

"I told you," she said, studying her wrecked manicure, "it doesn't make sense. It's too tangled up in all of my issues to approach sense."

"I suppose it makes as much sense as me being angry at myself. I had you on that desk when you presented me with the divorce papers and most of my anger was directed at me. For having a chance to have you, five long years to make love to you in any way I chose. Squandered. In the interest of control. Control I felt a deep conviction over, but that in the end I despised. You tell me how that makes sense."

"I can't tell you how. Only that it does. Because it mirrors much of what I feel."

"I think that's enough honesty for one evening,

don't you?" he asked, his tone growing hard suddenly, his dark eyes shuttered.

"I'm not done with the cookies," she said, taking another one out, this one dipped in chocolate.

"Then, I will wait. Because I find I'm not done with you."

"Oh," she said, putting the cookie back in the tin. Suddenly, she didn't care much about the cookie.

"Come on, *agape*. Let's go to bed."

Kairos had never spent the night with a woman. Not even his own wife. He questioned why he hadn't now. Because it was a thing of brilliant luxury. Luxury and satisfaction he had never known, to wake up with a soft, beautiful woman twined around his body. During their nap the evening before, they had not touched while they'd slept, but sometime during the night she had moved nearer to him, or he nearer to her. Her soft legs were laced through his.

Last night he'd had her more times than he could count. Every time he thought he was satisfied, desire would reach up again and grab him by the throat, compel him to have her. Another side effect of not sleeping with your wife was that intimacy was confined to a single moment. Something planned, something carefully orchestrated. There was always a definite start time. Then an end when he returned to his own bed.

The lines blurred when you didn't leave the room.

He found he quite liked the lines blurred.

He drew the covers back slightly, the pale morning light washing over her curves, revealing bruises on her skin. One on her back, four at her hips. His fingerprints.

He gritted his teeth, regret warring with arousal inside of him. There was something primal and masculine in him that celebrated the fact his mark remained. The fact that he had declared her his with these outward signs. She no longer wore his wedding ring, but she wore his touch like a brand.

What kind of monster was he?

"Tabitha," he asked, "are you awake?"

"No," she mumbled, rolling over onto her stomach, her blond hair falling over her face like a golden curtain. "If I were awake my eyes would be open."

His chest tightened, his stomach twisting. There was something charming about her like this. Not bound by her typical control, not conscious of the fact that she thought of him as little more than a stranger.

"You answered my question," he said.

"It would be rude not to," she muttered.

"I suppose that's true."

She turned over again, baring her breasts to his gaze, and he felt himself growing hard again.

She must be sore. He needed to practice restraint. He found he did not want to. For the first time in his life he was starting to think restraint was overrated. At least, where sex with one's wife was concerned.

"Why are you looking at me like that?" she asked, opening her eyes to a squint.

"Like what?"

"Like you want to…eat me. Or perhaps ask me deep questions."

"It is a bit early for either, I'm afraid. I require caffeine."

"I don't suppose I'm allowed to have very much caffeine," she said, her tone regretful.

"One cup of coffee will hurt nothing. Let's go downstairs."

"I have to get dressed."

"Why?"

She blinked. "I don't know. Because it seems like the thing to do?"

"Certainly don't dress on my account."

She shot him a deadly glare and got out of bed, crossing the room completely naked and making her way to the wardrobe. There was a white, silk robe in there, and she retrieved it, wrapping it over her curves much to his dismay. "This will do," she said.

"I suppose." He got out of bed, retrieving his pants from the night before and dragging them on, not bothering with underwear or his belt.

He had the strangest urge to pick her up and carry her downstairs, just as he had done when they'd gone upstairs last night. That made no sense. And if Kairos was anything, it was sensible. At least, he had been before the past few weeks. Impending fatherhood and divorce did that to a man, he supposed.

They made their way down the stairs in silence, setting about to prepare cereal and coffee, keeping it simple as both of them preferred to do. He was not accustomed to lingering over large breakfasts. Typically, he was eager to dive into his day. He realized now that he had abandoned the palace with only Andres in his stead, and very little explanation for why.

He dismissed the thought, for the first time in his life dismissing the weight of his responsibility.

That's what a spare was for, after all. To be used in cases of death, dismemberment or divorce. Divorce that needed to be stopped.

It was time Andres took his position a little bit more seriously anyway.

"And what plans have you made for us on this fine day," Tabitha asked, seated across from him at the table inside the dining area. He would have preferred to eat outside, but he had not yet cleaned up the mess of glass and food they had created last night. A drawback to not having staff in residence. The consequences of his actions were very much his own. Fine when he was engaging in normal activities. Less so when he was throwing his wife atop the most convenient surface and consigning anything in his way to the category of collateral damage.

"What makes you think I have some kind of grand plan?"

"Well, I would have thought my captor might be running the show."

"Your captor," he said. "I thought that we had moved beyond that."

"You are still holding me here, are you not?"

"You have agreed."

She sniffed. "Under sufferance."

"Oh, yes, your suffering is great. I believe I made you suffer a minimum of five times last night."

He was gratified to see her cheeks turn a deep shade of rose. A strange sense of satisfaction overtook him. He enjoyed her like this.

He did not think she was goading him because she was angry, not seriously. Rather, he had the feeling that she liked the sparks that crackled between them when they sparred. It was new. Like the unleashed sexual energy between them, this unveiled annoyance was new. Typically, they both buried their barbs much deeper.

"I didn't think a gentleman spoke to a lady in such a way," she said, her tone arch.

"I have found that being a gentleman is boring. Surely you must find being a lady similarly dull."

"In certain environments, yes."

"The bedroom being one of them."

"You may have a point." She lifted her coffee mug to her lips and took a sip. She turned her head, gazing out toward the ocean, the sun bathing her face in a warm glow. The corners of her lips turned up slightly, the breeze rippling through her blond hair.

It was a foreign moment, unlike any he'd had in recent memory. Where they were both relaxed. Companionable, even if only for a few moments.

"Perhaps we should go for a walk?"

"Not while I'm in my robe," she said.

"No. Of course not. But perhaps, you can look and see if my staff were so kind as to provide you with a swimsuit, and we could go down to the ocean."

"We never do things like this."

"I know. But this is the time for us to explore things we've never done. That is the purpose."

"Yes, so you said. I just didn't think it extended to long walks on the beach."

"Why not? Perhaps you will discover we enjoy it. Perhaps it is something we will want to do with our child."

Her smile turned sad. "You do play dirty."

"I will play however I must. If I can make myself seem indispensable to your vision of a happy family, then I'll win. I'm not above using any means necessary."

"I did not take you for being cutthroat, Kairos."

"I hide it well. I rarely need to use it. My title insulates me from much pushback. From much criticism at all. Even if it exists, the teeth aren't sharp enough to do me any harm."

"Will *you* be wearing a swimsuit? I'm wondering if I can look forward to a show."

"I suppose it would be impractical of me to attempt to swim without one."

"Okay, now I'm starting to fear that you've been body snatched. My husband is talking about spending leisure time on the beach. And also, participating in recreational activity."

"No, sadly for you, I remain Kairos. I have not been snatched and replicated by a more biddable man. But if nothing else, I hope this proves to you that even if it is not in my nature to behave a certain way, I can try to change. I can try to accommodate your needs, even if I don't understand them perfectly."

She nodded slowly, and he had a feeling that she found something in his speech unsatisfactory. But then, that was not terribly unusual.

"All right, I'm going to go change. I'll meet you back down here," he said. Because if he joined her in her room, they would never leave.

Not that he minded. But he supposed it ran counter to appealing to her emotions.

"All right. Let's see if either of us can rise to the challenge of being leisurely."

Whoever had done the shopping for Tabitha's wardrobe deserved a raise. That was all Kairos could think as he walked behind her on the beach, taking in the sight of all the bare skin that was on display for his enjoyment. It was a white bikini, one that scarcely contained her perfect figure. The sort of thing she would never have worn on a regular basis.

But this was not a regular basis. This was outside the status quo. And he meant to take advantage of that.

For the moment, that meant admiring Tabitha in her bikini.

"You're staring at me," she said, not looking back at him.

"How do you know?" he asked, feeling a stirring of humor in his chest.

Such a rare feeling. He felt light, happy almost. Yes, things were unsettled between them, but the chemistry they were exploring was off the charts. And right now, he was on a pristine, private beach and she was barely clothed. There was nothing to dislike about the moment.

"I can feel you looking," she said.

"I was not aware you had a sixth sense, *agape*. I learn more secrets about you every moment."

"I don't have all that many."

He caught up to her, keeping pace with her strides. "But you do have some?"

"I told you the biggest one," she said, the humor leaching from her tone as she said those words.

"Are there more? Surely there must be. You are not defined by one traumatic event. Tell me. I want to know more about you."

"I was born in Iowa."

"I don't know anything about Iowa."

She laughed. "No one does. Join the club."

"Did you like it there?"

She laughed. "Do I still live there, Kairos?"

"No. But one cannot be the queen of Iowa. So I suppose in your case, you did not have to *dislike* it to leave."

"The queen of Iowa does have a nice ring to it, though."

"Perhaps not as elegant as the queen of Petras."

"Perhaps not."

He leaned closer to her, taking her hand in his, pausing for a moment when she went stiff beside him. "Tell me more."

"My mother was single until I was eight. Then

she married my stepfather. You know how that ended. It was… It was not all bad. She wasn't. He wasn't. He was…the only father figure I ever had. He was kind to me." She closed her eyes. "I remember once he bought me a present for…no reason. My mother never did things like that." Her eyes fluttered open again. "But they were very wrapped up in each other, and I was an only child. Mostly, it was lonely."

"What about friends? Didn't you have friends?"

"Some. People studying advanced subjects in school. Other students who actually enjoyed getting good grades." She paused, a fine line creasing her brow. "Someone came to speak at the school when I was young. A doctor. She had grown up in the area, with no money, nothing. It was a very poor town, and seeing someone come out of it and do what she did was inspiring. She told us that if we worked hard enough we can all achieve it. She talked to us about scholarships. About the kinds of things we could hope to find if we needed to succeed on merit rather than on status or money. I felt like she was speaking to me. I was smart, but we had nothing. My resources were all inside of me. And I was determined to use them. It was all I was given on this earth. I didn't want to waste them."

"From where I'm standing, I would say you didn't." How had he ever seen this woman as soft? She was pure steel. Brave as hell. She was braver than he was, truth be told. All he'd done was fall into line with what was expected of him. She had defied expectation at every turn. Had been brought into this world with no opportunity and from it had fashioned herself into royalty. He imagined there were very few people who could say the same.

"But you don't get into good universities without hard work," she said.

"I would imagine not. I got in with a pedigree."

"People do, but I got in by being exceptional. I had to be. There's so much competition for scholarships. Especially the type I needed. Full rides. Living expenses paid. I needed every bit of help I could scrounge up for myself. My mother went to prison for killing my stepfather during my last year of school. But I just…kept working. I was so close to being eighteen, social services sort of let me be. And I…stayed in the house by myself."

"Tabitha…" His heart ached for her. For this woman who had been so lonely for so long.

"It was all right. I mean, it wasn't in some ways, but in others… I could study in peace. I just kept going to school. And when I got to university, keeping what I had was dependent on maintaining a near-perfect grade point average. I could never afford to have boyfriends. Couldn't waste any time or energy on parties. I had to be single-minded. And I was."

"And a year into school you decided to move to Petras to take a job as my assistant," he said. "Why exactly?"

"As I said, I wasn't after a university experience. I wasn't about making friends. I wanted to secure my future. The internship allowed me to complete my classes, and to gain the kind of work experience that most people would give a body part away to acquire. To work for the royal family? For someone with my background that's more valuable than money. That's a connection.

The kind of connection someone like me can't typically hope to ever obtain."

"And then you married me instead."

"You made me an offer I couldn't refuse."

His heart expanded, a sense of fullness pervading his chest. He could hardly breathe. "You're very brave, Tabitha. I never fully appreciated that."

She looked down, tucking a strand of hair behind her ear. "I don't know if I'm especially brave. I was just more afraid of repeating the same life I'd already had as a child than I was of striking out on my own and failing."

"I've heard it said that courage isn't the absence of fear."

"No. Without fear we would not move very fast."

"Is that why you were running from me?"

She frowned, turning away from him and continuing on down the beach. For some reason that action pushed a long-ignored memory to the front of his mind.

"Don't go." He was twelve years old. He might as well be a man. He never cried. And yet, he could

feel emotion closing down hard on his throat, strange prickling feeling pushing at the backs of his eyes.

The hall was empty except for him and his mother. He knew that she wasn't simply going out for a walk. She didn't have anything in her hand beyond her purse. But still, he knew. As certain as if she had announced it, he knew that this was the last time he would ever see her.

"Stay here, Kairos," she said, her voice steady. If there was any regret inside of her, she certainly wasn't showing it.

"You can't go," he said, calling on his most commanding tone. Of course, his voice chose that exact moment to crack in two, as it had been doing with increasing frequency lately. "I am the prince," he continued, drawing strength from deep within him. "I forbid you."

She paused, turning to face him, the expression in her eyes unfathomably sad. "It will end eventually, whether I leave now or not. Do you think I have anything your father wanted? No. But he wanted you. He wanted Andres. In that way, I didn't fail. Remind him of that when he's raging about this tomorrow."

She turned away from him again, continuing down the long hallway. And he forgot to be brave. Forgot that he was supposed to be a man.

A cry escaped his lips and he ran after her, wrapping his arms around her, pressing his head against her back and inhaling the familiar scent of her. Honey and tuberose, mixed with the powder she applied to her face.

His cheeks were wet, tears falling easily now. "Don't go. I won't give you orders again. I'm begging you, please don't leave. Mom, please."

She rested her hands against his forearms, then curled her fingers around his wrist. She pushed down hard, extricating herself from his hold. "I have to."

And then she walked away from him. At the palace door.

And he never saw her again.

He was breathing hard, his chest burning, his brain swimming with memories he usually kept locked down deep.

And then he looked at Tabitha.

He was treading on dangerous ground with her. He wasn't neutral. And this wasn't strictly sexual. It never had been.

Dammit. He had to get it together. He needed this time to convince her to stay with him. But he would never, ever be…that again. Never again would he allow himself to feel so much for someone that the loss of them would break him.

Never again would he be reduced to shameful begging in his own home to keep a woman with him.

He was different now. Harder. He was the man his father had commanded him to be. Not the boy who'd clung to a woman who felt nothing for him and wept as though his heart were breaking.

"I didn't work years to improve my position in life only to settle for an existence that makes me unhappy."

"What does happiness have to do with anything?" Kairos asked. "Happiness is just a socially acceptable word for selfishness. We all talk about how we need to be happy. About how our happiness must come first. In which case, leaving her husband and children isn't abominable. It's brave. Because you were only preserving your own happiness, am I right?"

"That isn't true."

Anger fired through his blood, the memory of his mother walking away still at the forefront of his mind, superimposing itself over this moment. Over this woman. "Of course it is. You can wander off into the far reaches of the world and eat, pray, love to your heart's content regardless of who you leave behind because you're on a journey to your essential truth and damn anyone else's."

"That isn't what I'm doing. We were both drowning in that marriage, don't pretend we weren't."

"I have a feeling we might have drowned either way," he said.

"I'm trying. I said I would try. Must you make this unpleasant?"

He had a feeling that he must. Fighting with her did something to ease the swollen feeling in his chest. And he found he was much more comfortable with anger than he was with anything tender or painful.

There was nothing wrong with attempting to forge a stronger physical connection between the two of them. But he needed to remember who he was. What his responsibilities were. And what they wanted. He could not afford to be preoccupied with her in any emotional sense.

He had to maintain control while making her lose it.

Had to find a way to convince her to stay with him while maintaining the distance he required.

He had imagined that global distance would be beneficial. That it would prevent his wife from leaving him. He had been wrong. He needed distance. She had to need him.

"My apologies, *agape*," he said. "I'm much more useful when it comes to interacting with heads of state than I am with making pleasant conversation."

"I'm not sure I have very much practice with casual conversation myself."

"That could be a problem. I'm given to understand that children like to make conversation about very small things. Such as insects and the shapes of clouds."

A strange, soft expression passed over her face and had made his heart clench tight. "Well, I have very little to say on the subject of insects. But I do think that cloud looks like a unicorn."

He moved so that he was standing beside her, oriented so that he was facing the same direction she was. "I don't see it."

"What do you see?"

"A war horse. With a lance growing out of his forehead."

"That's a unicorn."

"Clearly, we have different perspectives on things."

Then she smiled, and he thought that he must be doing something right. As long as he continued on, insulating himself against any sort of attachment beyond the practical, he would be able to bind her to him.

He had been blinded by the sex. By the unexpected connection it had provided. But now, in the bright light of day, when she was not on her knees before him, offering up the most tempting image and indulgence he had ever experienced, he had a bit more clarity.

His path was clear. And he would allow nothing to make them deviate from it.

CHAPTER TEN

KAIROS HAD ANOTHER romantic dinner prepared for them out on the terrace. It was dark, the stars in the sky shining brightly as warm air mingled and cooled with mist from the sea, and washed over her skin as she closed her eyes, taking a moment to enjoy the beauty of it. Of what it felt like to be here.

There were only nine days left. Nine days until she had to make a decision about whether or not she was going to leave him. But then, she wasn't entirely sure there was a decision to be made.

Yes, she could have his money if she left after fulfilling the terms of his bargain. But she was starting to think that would be nowhere near enough. Neither would shared custody. Because in that scenario she wouldn't get to be with him. She would never see what kind of father he was to their child. Her child would have a life divided in half. She would never be able to watch the way he interacted with Kairos. Would never be able to fully understand what his life at the palace was like.

Right now, tiny as it was, her baby lived inside of her. She couldn't imagine relinquishing so much time with him once he was born.

She realized that yet again, she was worrying about the future. Existing in the present, but only by half. She had spent her entire life that way. Living for a moment she wasn't yet in. It struck her, suddenly and sharply.

"I don't know if I've ever really been happy before," she said, looking up from her plate and meeting his gaze.

He looked at her, his expression guarded. He had been a bit more cautious with her since their walk on the beach the other day. Had not been quite so relaxed. Initially, she had attributed it to some kind of leisure fatigue on his part. She had rarely seen Kairos being anything but the stately ruler with posture so stiff he would make a military general envious. Now she wondered. It was something else.

But unless he told her, she wouldn't know. That, right there, was the summation of their entire relationship.

"Another bit of commentary on my skills as a husband?" he asked, his tone dry.

"No. Commentary on myself. I'm always thinking ahead. No matter where I was, it was never enough. It's never been enough. I arrive at a goal-post and I'm immediately looking ahead to the next. I spent all of high school anticipating how I would get into a university. Then I spent all that time calculating my next move. Spent every moment of my internship with you figuring out how I would parlay that into a fabulous gold star on my résumé, what job I would get when it was finished. And then, by the strangest twist of fate I could ever have imagined, I ended up being queen of the nation. I have no goal beyond that, Kairos. You can't go up from there. I was—and am—at the very top. Secure for life, in a position where I can make a difference in the world. And I've still never been happy."

"I was born a prince, I'm not certain I've ever been particularly happy about it," he said, his tone hard. "But we are in a position to do much good. Isn't that more important than happiness?"

"I suppose. As is security. Or at least, in my experience it's difficult to be happy without security. But… Don't you think it's possible to have happiness as well?"

"I don't give it much thought."

"I think for me I've never allowed myself to rest because of the fear."

He froze then, his dark eyes flat. "Is that so?"

"Yes. I don't…I don't think I've ever honestly feared that I would turn into my mother. You're right, Kairos. I never feared that I would actually pick up a gun and shoot you in a jealous rage. But I… Attachments frighten me. How do you know who you can trust? She was my mother. She raised me from the cradle. I never imagined she would do something like that. I never saw it coming. How do you… I have always struggled to figure out how you trust someone after that. I knew her longer than I had known anyone, and still, she did something so far outside of what I imagined she might be capable of."

"I do understand something of that. It might

have escaped your notice but my trust has been betrayed a time or two in my life."

Guilt twisted her stomach, because she knew that she was part of that now. A part of the betrayals that he had experienced.

"I've been thinking a lot about it. A lot about happiness. About trust. I've been waiting to feel a magical sense of both for a very long time. For my position in life to hand me happiness, for time to grant me trust of the situation I'm in. Neither has come. And so, I'm left with only one conclusion."

"That is?"

"I have to choose it. I'm going to have to make a decision to be content. I mean, for the love of God, I'm a queen with a handsome husband, a private island, a palace and a baby on the way. Choosing happiness should not be that difficult. But I think in order to achieve that I'm going to have to choose trust as well. I've been so reluctant to do that. Because the idea of having my trust misused scares me. The idea of trusting *myself* scares me. But…I can't predict the future. Neither can I control you. I can't control any of the circumstances around us, all I can do is make choices for myself. If I want to trust you, then I have to decide to trust you." She looked down, then back up again. "Trust is just like happiness. You can't wait for the evidence. Then it isn't trust. You have to choose it. And be ready to be damned along with that choice if it comes to it. But I trust you."

"So simple, *agape*?"

"Why not? So many things in life are hard. We have no control over them. I know you're well familiar with that too. Who can dictate the things that live inside of us if not us? Why do we look around, trying to claim dominion over things we cannot, while we let the things we could dominate us?"

"I didn't realize I was going to get psychology with my meal."

"I thought it paired nicely with the fish, as we can't have wine."

"And here I thought anthropology went better with fish."

"Not my field of expertise."

"A disappointment," he said. "You always seem expert in everything you try."

"Everything?" she asked, arching a brow.

His gaze turned hot. "Yes," he said, his voice rough now. "Everything."

"Hmm. Well, but then, you haven't got much experience with some of what we've been doing." She had a feeling she was edging into forbidden territory, but she wanted to ask him about this.

"This is true," he said.

"You were not a virgin when we married."

He paused, his fork halfway between the plate and his mouth. "No," he said.

"So it isn't inexperience that caused you to go without a woman...without...what I gave you recently."

"True. Are you really in the mood to examine my past relationships?"

"No," she said. "Not especially. I only want to know why. I mean, you had sex with other women but not...not that. Is it control?"

He set his fork down. "I...I'm not certain how to answer that."

"With the truth. Not your carefully reasoned

version, or what you think I might want to hear. Or even what you think makes sense. The real reason. The truth."

He looked as though she'd hit him, and for a second, she felt sorry for him. But not much beyond a second. "I never felt like I deserved such a thing." The words fell from his lips reluctantly, and she could tell that even he was mystified by them.

"Why?" she asked.

"I've never liked the idea of sitting back and taking something like that as my due. You can't… You have to earn things. And serve. You can never just…take."

"I mean, I agree. Reciprocation and being generous is certainly appreciated, but what does that have to do with letting your partner show you she wants you?"

"I've never felt I could afford such a thing. To give in to such selfish desire," he said, uncomfortable now. Clearly.

"Don't you think now after so many years… don't you think you might deserve something for you, Kairos?"

He curled his hand into a fist and she watched the tendons there shift. Everything about him was so strong. So beautiful. "Are you through eating?" he asked.

"Yes."

"I find that I am ready for bed."

Her heart fluttered, excitement firing through her body. She never tired of this new, more physically attentive Kairos. He didn't bother to hold back the attraction that burned between them. This was sex for the sole purpose of forging a deeper connection between them, finding pleasure with each other, rather than timing their unions around her cycle. It was an entirely different experience, and she loved it.

"Then, I am too," she said, without hesitation.

It occurred to her, as he swept her into his arms and carried her away from the terrace, that he might have been redirecting the conversation. That he was replacing the promise of honest talk with sex.

But she wouldn't allow those thoughts to poison the moment. She had chosen happiness. She had chosen trust. And so, she would cling to those things, as she clung to him.

In his arms, it wasn't difficult to feel perfectly content in the present. To feel secure.

And to trust that everything would work out in the end.

In spite of her resolution to trust more, she found herself overtaken with a sense of disquiet over the next couple of days. Kairos was definitely distancing himself again. She had lived under the carefully constructed frost blanket he preferred to lay out over everything for too many years not to recognize when he was gearing up to roll it out again. He made love with her every night, yes, but she didn't wake up held securely in his arms as she had done initially here on the island.

Instead, she awoke with a yawning stretch of space between them. He slept on the side of the bed nearest the door, and she couldn't help but think that one morning she would wake up and he would have gone completely. As though he were inching ever closer to the exit with each passing night.

Trust, she reasoned, was not blind stupidity. Trust was going to have to extend to herself as well, not just to him. She had to trust her own instincts where he was concerned. Something had changed, and it wasn't anything good. It was reverting back.

She couldn't help but wonder if he had gotten too close to that fire she talked about earlier, and was running from it now. If all of the intimacy, not just the sex, was getting to him. For the first time, they had really begun to talk. To peel back the layers beneath their clothes and look at who they were, not who they pretended to be.

This thing between them was uncomfortable. That much she knew. It always had been. That was why they had both turned away from it so resolutely.

She was done with that. Sadly for him, she wasn't going to allow him to run.

They had less than a week. Less than a week to fix this thing between them. She wanted to stay with him. She had made that decision. But she wanted their marriage to be something more. She was not going to determine to remain his wife only to have things revert back to their icy state.

No, she was going to effect change. Permanent change.

Conversation didn't seem to work with him. The only way through to Kairos seemed to be using her body. When he decided to transform her from personal assistant to wife, it had been because of her mind. Because they connected on a logical level.

She was done appealing to logic. She was going to make the appeal with her body. She was going to come at all of this from a different direction. She wondered now if she had tried to seduce him sooner if things would have changed before she walked out.

There was no denying the heat that shimmered between them.

But intimacy had been missing from their sexual encounters in the past. Honesty had been missing.

She intended to reach for both tonight. To strip him bare completely, not just of his clothes, but everything else.

She had dug into the back of that wardrobe, every piece of clothing provided her by a stranger, and found a bright red dress that she would normally never have chosen. She felt as though it was painted over her curves, clinging so tightly to everything, she was certain that each and every flaw her body claimed as its own was on very loud display.

She had never worried terribly much about her figure. Why, when her husband spent so little time looking at it? But now, she intended to use it as a weapon. To be sufficient ammunition to blast that mountain of a man down to his knees.

She took a breath and looked at herself in the mirror. She hardly recognized the woman she saw there. Her blond hair was spilling over her shoulders, unrestrained. She had not styled it within an inch of its life, had not tamed it into submission. Rather, it looked a little bit wild. She was wearing lipstick that matched the dress, also much bolder and brighter than she tended to be.

But a seduction of this importance required bold and bright.

She walked down the sweeping staircase, her

fingertips skimming the rail. She had repainted her nails to match the dress and to get rid of the chipped polish she had been wearing for the past few days. She wasn't going to nervously pick at this manicure. In part, because she wasn't going to be nervous.

She gritted her teeth, repeating that mantra over and over again. As though, if she thought it enough times it would make it true.

Then she saw Kairos, standing at the foot of the stairs, wearing a white shirt that was unbuttoned at his throat, revealing a tempting wedge of bronzed skin, just a hint of his dark chest hair. She loved his chest. Could spend hours exploring it with her hands, her lips and her tongue. She found that she had very few inhibitions where he was concerned. That, at least, had made the past week fun.

She smiled as her foot hit the floor and she stood, waiting to see if she could discern his reaction to her appearance.

He was stoic, as ever, his expression schooled into hard granite. But it was that grim set of his mouth, that determination in his eyes that let her know that he was in fact affected. His jaw was so tight, the veins in his neck were standing out, his hands clenched into fists, the enticing muscles of his forearms flexed with the strength that it took for him to restrain himself.

Yes, she was certainly having an effect.

"Are you dressed for dinner?" he asked.

"Actually, I'm dressed for dessert."

Kairos was not entirely certain when he lost control of the situation. Whether it was the moment he caught sight of Tabitha descending the stairs in that dress that clung to her body like a lover, outlining her full breasts, slim waist and perfectly rounded hips. Whether it was when his eyes zeroed in on her lips, painted a bold red, and he immediately imagined her leaving that color all over his skin.

Or whether it was sometime much earlier. Whether it had been slowly sifting through his fingers like sand through an hourglass from the moment they first arrived on this island. He had brought her here to force her to come around to his way of thinking. But standing here, his world seemingly turned on end, he was beginning to wonder who was in charge.

She closed the distance between them, pressing her breasts against his chest, curling her fingers around the back of his neck and drawing his head down for a kiss. It was slow, achingly so. He wanted to wrap her in his embrace, crush her up against him and claim her completely. To show her that she was not the one in control here. But he didn't want this to end. He was so desperate to see what she had planned.

Even while everything in him denied it.

Distancing himself from Tabitha over the past few days had not been a simple task. He had tasted paradise, unrestrained, unmitigated bliss at her hands, and then he had put up a wall. Had drawn a veil between them, blunting their every interaction since. Not allowing himself to get lost in it, not completely, not again. He knew his reasoning was sound, but it was a torture that he had not counted on.

She flicked her tongue out, tracing the edge of his upper lip slowly. Heat fired along his veins, molten fire pooling in his stomach. And he almost lost his control completely in that moment. She pressed her palm against his chest, against where his heart raged, almost out of control, then slid her fingertips down over his stomach, to his belt buckle. She looked up, her eyes meeting his, and his breath caught in his throat.

She meant to do this slow, that he could see clearly. It also might kill him, that he could see clearly too.

She worked his belt through the loop slowly, an echo to that first time she had gone down on him out on the terrace. She finished undoing the clasp on his pants, slipped her hands beneath the fabric and curled her delicate fingers around his aching flesh. His breath hissed through his teeth, his entire body going rigid beneath her touch.

She deepened her kiss as she stroked him, mirroring the rhythm of her hand with her tongue. An involuntary shudder wracked his entire body and she squeezed him tightly as she bit his lower lip.

"Tabitha," he growled. Begging. Cursing. Warning.

"What?" she asked, her tone a model of innocence.

"Do not test me," he said, not even knowing entirely what he meant. Only that he was desperate to push her away, but he wasn't strong enough. Physically, of course he was strong enough. She was a soft, petite woman, and physically he could overpower her if he chose. It was his spirit that wasn't strong enough. He was powerless beneath her touch. And if one of them was going to make the choice to walk away from this moment, it would have to be her. Because he could not. He had tried over the past few days to practice restraint and he was all out of it.

Not just the past few days, the past five years. Five long years of being married to a woman such as her and holding his desire for her in check. He could not. He could not endure the restraint any longer.

"Oh, *agape*, I have come here to test you. And I hope very much you fail," she said, angling her head and kissing his neck, her teeth scraping the sensitive skin there. "I came here to give myself to you. As a gift. One without strings. One you can use as selfishly as you wish. You can enjoy this, enjoy me, to your heart's content."

A feral sound escaped his lips, and he tightened his hold on her, sliding his hands down her thighs and lifting her up, her dress riding up past her hips, her legs wrapped around his waist as he carried her from the base of the stairs into the living area.

He moved over to the couch, lowering himself down onto it, keeping a hold of her hips. He sat, with her straddling his lap, her arms wrapped around his neck, his grip on her tight. She arched against him, pressing the heat of her against his heart and arousal, a short, luxurious sound of pleasure resonating through her as she did.

"I like this view," he said, sliding his hand up her waist and moving it to cup her breast, teasing her nipple with his thumb. "It is a beautiful dress. But I think I would prefer it on the floor."

He reached around, taking hold of the zipper tab and drawing it downward, letting the dress fall around her waist, revealing pale, perfect breasts. He leaned in, lowering his head and drawing one tightened bud into his mouth before circling it slowly with the tip of his tongue. She shivered beneath his touch and a surge of satisfaction claimed him. Stole every thought from his mind. He could think of nothing else but having her, consuming her, giving her mindless pleasure as she had done for him.

He tightened his hold on her, reversing their positions so that she was sitting down on the couch and he was overhead. He lowered himself onto the floor, grabbing hold of her dress and pulling it from her body, finding her completely bare beneath it. He swore, lowering himself further so that he was down on his knees, a supplicant worshipping at the temple of her beauty.

She was so beautiful, so perfectly aroused and uninhibited for him. He was so hard it was a physical pain. He wanted nothing more than to free himself completely from his clothes and bury himself deep inside of her.

But then it would be over. Far too quickly. And she was not half so mindless as he needed her to be.

He realized then that this was the definition of being thoroughly seduced. To the degree that Tabitha was no longer even the aggressor. His body was convinced that this was absolutely his idea and that there was no other course of action. He was not going to fight against it.

He moved his hands slowly along her inner thighs, avoiding the most feminine part of her. Relishing it when she shifted beneath his touch, a needy, disappointed sound escaping from her as he avoided the place he knew she was desperate for him to touch.

"Kairos," she said, her tone holding a hint of steel. A hint of demand.

"Patience, *agape*," he said.

"Why?" she asked, "I've waited five years for you to look at me like this. Why should I wait another moment?"

She was not wrong. He had never done this for her before. Had never tasted her.

He regretted it bitterly.

But he would not allow the regret to linger for much longer. Because he would satisfy that desire soon. Would satiate his appetite for her. But only after he had made her beg for it.

He moved his hand between her thighs, his finger gliding through her slick flesh, over the bundle of nerves there. She arched her back, letting her head fall back, thrusting her breasts forward, her chest rising and falling quickly with her sharp, uncontrolled breaths.

He teased the entrance to her body with his fingertips, spurred on by every restless shift of her hips as she sought out deeper penetration. "You want me," he said, his voice so rocky he barely recognized it. "You really want me."

"Yes," she gasped. "Kairos, stop teasing me."

"So wet for me, my sweet wife. I know you didn't marry me because of any passion between us. But you *do* want me." He didn't know why he felt compelled to hear her say it. To hear her confirm it yet again. Perhaps because she had left him. Perhaps because he knew she had been unhappy for so long. Because he knew he had not satisfied her physical needs as well as he could have.

Because he needed to know, beyond a shadow of a doubt that he was not alone in this deep, howling need that overtook him completely. That made him feel restless and needy. That made him feel as though he would die if he was denied her.

Forget oxygen, Tabitha was the most essential element for his survival.

And he needed to know that he wasn't alone.

"I want you," she said.

"More than you have ever wanted another man?"

"I have *never* wanted another man. You're the only one. The only man I've ever kissed. The only one I've ever touched."

On a feral growl, he moved his hands, gripping her hips hard and tugging her toward the edge of the couch as he lowered his head, tasting her deeply, all semblance of restrained seduction gone completely. He was starving for her. And she was the sweetest dessert he had ever conceived of. He had been a fool to have her all these years and never have her in this way. He had been a fool to have her in his life, in his bed, and to hold himself back from her.

He was lost in her, lost in this. Lost in the needy sounds she made, in the sweet, soft surrender of her entire body. She shuddered beneath him as release overtook her. And still, he didn't stop. Didn't stop until she was sobbing, until she was begging, until another climax overtook her and she was trembling.

"I can't," she said, her tone spent.

"You can," he said, not sure where his confidence came from, not certain how he could make such a proclamation about her body. Only that in this moment, he felt as though he owned a part of it. A part of her. "You will." He kissed her inner thigh before rising up and wrapping his arm around her waist, lowering her down onto her back and positioning himself over her. "I need you," he said, kissing her lips deeply as he thrust into her.

She cried out, arching up against him, pressing her breasts against his chest, pushing her hips up against his as he buried himself inside of her. She met his every movement with one of her own, met each kiss, each sound of pleasure.

He tried to go slow, tried to keep things measured, controlled. But he was beyond any of that now. Beyond anything but his intense need for her. Arousal roared through his veins like a beast, overtaking him, consuming him. And he gave up on control. Gave up on slow. On gentle or restrained. He slipped his hands beneath her bottom, drawing her up hard against him as he thrust in deep. As he increased the intensity, as he let the world fade away, he lost himself completely in the tight, wet heat of her body.

Her internal muscles clenched tightly around him, and he felt another orgasm radiating through her. It called irresistibly to the beast inside of him. As though it was just the thing he had been waiting for. It grabbed him by the throat and he could do nothing but submit to it. To the wild, unquenchable pleasure that gripped him tightly and shook him until he was left there, bleeding out on the ground, completely and utterly defeated by the strength of the desire that had claimed him.

When it was over, he realized where he was. Naked, utterly vulnerable, utterly claimed by the woman beneath him.

He had no walls up, no defenses.

And it was unacceptable.

He pushed away from her, forcing his fingers through his hair, resting his elbows on his thighs as he leaned forward, trying to catch his breath.

"Kairos?" Her voice was soft, questioning,

and he hated himself for the bastard that he was. Hated that she was now asking for things that he could never give.

And it was his fault. Because he had given in to her. Because he had sought to bind her to him while knowing he would never be able to give all of himself. Still, even feeling like the lowest form of life on the planet, he knew he could do nothing else. He knew there was no other course of action to be taken. He needed her. Needed her in his life forever, and at the same time he knew his own weaknesses. Knew that he had to keep his defenses strong.

This could not be endured.

"Thank you for a lovely dessert, Tabitha," he said, rising to his feet. "I find I am in need of a bit of solitude."

He rose to his feet.

"Kairos," she said, her voice shaky. "Stay."

It was all so familiar. So blindingly, painfully familiar. In this scenario, she was the boy he'd been, abandoned, shunned.

And he had become the one leaving.

No. He was doing this for her. To spare her any

more pain. To spare himself, the country, from what might happen if he were to ever surrender to his own base needs.

He was not the villain here. Even if she couldn't see it now.

He turned away from her, walking from the room. And no matter how much he burned to take one last look at her, he refused. Denied himself now as he should have done from the first.

He had been weak tonight. He would not be so again.

CHAPTER ELEVEN

"Kairos?"

The sound of Tabitha's voice pierced Kairos's sleep. He had gone back to his room after their encounter in the living room, and he had stayed there for the rest of the evening. At some point, in spite of his discomfort, he must have fallen asleep.

"What?" he asked, not quite awake enough to sort through whether or not it was strange she was waking him up in the middle of the night.

"Kairos," she said, again. There was something in her voice that jolted him completely into wakefulness. Something tremulous, something terrified.

"What is it?"

"I'm bleeding." The word ended on a sob. "Kairos, I'm bleeding."

He shot out of bed, giving no thought to

clothes, giving no thought to anything but figuring out what was happening. "What do you mean you're…?" It hit him then, exactly what it meant. "The baby."

He flipped the light on, and got a look at her face, her eyes large, her skin waxen. He had never seen Tabitha look quite like this. It occurred to him then that *she* might also be in danger. "How much blood?"

"Enough."

"How do you feel?"

"Terrified."

"I meant do you feel like you've lost too much blood?"

Her eyes grew rounder still. "Too much blood for someone who's having a baby."

"I need to call someone," he said. In that moment, his brain was blank, and he had no idea who to call. Why could he think of nothing? He was renowned for being cool under pressure. He was king of an entire nation, after all. But everything he knew, everything he thought, everything he felt was wrapped up in utter terror.

A helicopter. They needed a helicopter.

That jolted him out of his frozen state, and he reached for the phone that was sitting on his nightstand, dialing his right-hand man of the palace with one touch. "The queen is having an emergency," he said, his voice frayed. "We need a helicopter. Now. Medical personnel onboard would be ideal, but if that isn't possible, speed is more important."

"Of course, Your Highness," his man said. "We should be able to send one from the closest island and have you back in Petras in less than an hour. Further instructions will be texted to you, as far as where you should wait to be picked up."

Kairos hung up the phone, looking toward Tabitha. "Help will be here soon," he said.

She only looked at him with very large eyes, and he realized how empty and useless his words were. "Will it be too late?"

Suddenly, all of his power, his title, his status, meant nothing. Everything he had worked his entire life to become was reduced to useless ash. He didn't know the answer to the only question that mattered. He had no control over the outcome of the only thing Tabitha cared about in this moment. He could be a king, or he could be a homeless man, standing on a street corner begging for change. It wouldn't make a difference in this moment. Never before had he been so aware of his own failings. Of his own limitations.

"I don't know," he said, hating himself for not having a better answer.

She closed the distance between them, collapsing against him. He wrapped his arms around her, holding her against him, feeling unworthy that she was seeking comfort in his arms. He had nothing concrete to give her. He was of no use.

The minutes stretched on, a concrete bit of evidence of the relativity of time. It felt like hours since he had made that phone call. He found a pair of pants for himself, but bothered with nothing else. He would need to be decent when the helicopter arrived, but he could not take the time to cover more than society demanded.

Tabitha said nothing. Periodically, she would make a small, distressed sound that would pierce his heart and send a wave of pain through his body. The silence, the endless minutes, gave him plenty of opportunity to reflect on the evening. On his actions.

He had lost his control. He had been rough with her, little more than an animal. And now this. Surely it could not be a coincidence. It was a direct result of him losing himself. Losing sight of what he must be. Of what was important. In pursuit of his own emotions, he had compromised her. Their future. The future of the entire kingdom. Five years, and this was the only time they had ever successfully conceived a child, and now they were losing it.

Because of him.

Because he had become everything he despised.

At that moment his phone vibrated, and he looked down and saw a message giving instructions on where they were to meet the helicopter. "Hold on," he said, scooping Tabitha up into his arms and carrying her down the stairs, outside into the windy night. The approaching helicopter whipped the trees brutally, the sound thundering through his body. "Hold on," he said again, unsure whether she could hear him over the noise.

The giant machine touched down, and Kairos crossed the space, Tabitha held securely in his arms. Too little too late. Everything he was doing now was too little too late.

He got inside the helicopter, never releasing his hold on Tabitha. "Is anyone in here a medical professional?" The pilot and the only other men inside the cockpit shook their heads. "Then just fly as quickly as you can."

Tabitha felt weak, dazed. But then, she imagined an emergency, early-morning helicopter flight and all of the emotional trauma that had gone with it was bound to leave anyone feeling weak and dazed.

She had been in the hospital for a couple of hours now, waiting on results. She'd gotten an ultrasound, but of course the tech hadn't been able to tell her much of anything. She had to wait for the doctor. And they were also waiting for results of her blood work.

She had dozed off and on. Kairos, as far she could tell, had not even sat down since they'd arrived. She wanted to believe it was concern for her, but after the way he had distanced himself from her last night, she had serious doubts about that. A sinking feeling settled over her, dragging her down. As if she had much farther down to go.

Just then, the door to the hospital room opened and the doctor came in.

"Queen Tabitha," she said, her voice soft. "King Kairos. I'm very sorry to see you at such a stressful time."

A distressed sound filled the room, and Tabitha realized it had come from her. Hearing apology on the doctor's lips had sent a sharp, piercing pain through her. If the doctor was sorry, there was no good news for her. No good news for her baby.

"Your Majesty," the doctor said, "don't lose faith. I don't love the results that I have in front of me, but they could be worse. We were not able to see a heartbeat on the sonogram. But you have not miscarried. There is definitely something. It could very well be that it is just too early to see anything yet. Your hCG levels are quite low. I'm hoping that in a week's time we will be able to see the heartbeat, and that these levels will have doubled, which will give us an indication for how viable the pregnancy is."

Tabitha's ears were ringing. The words the doctor had just spoken were rattling around in her head, as she made an attempt to translate them.

"So she hasn't lost the baby," Kairos said, moving to stand nearer to her hospital bed.

"No," the doctor said, "at least, she hasn't miscarried. It's impossible for us to determine whether or not the fetus is viable at this point."

A tear rolled down Tabitha's cheek. She wanted the doctor to be angry, to be upset, and she knew that was counter to anything helpful. Still, she felt as if the world was falling apart. The least everyone around her could do was look as if they could see that. Like they could feel it too. Instead of throwing around all these technical terms with a calm, clinical tone that set her teeth on edge.

"Well, that's good," Kairos said, his tone as modified as the doctor's.

"The bleeding could have easily been the result of a blood vessel rupture, and might not indicate any serious issue at all."

"Until then…" Kairos spoke. "Should she be on bed rest? Should she be doing anything special?"

"If she's going to miscarry, at this stage bed rest won't help. Whatever activity she feels up to should be okay." The doctor finally turned her attention to Tabitha. "Get rest when you feel you need it. Sleep as much as you need to. Just listen to your body."

"I'm sort of angry at my body at the moment," Tabitha said. "It isn't doing what it's supposed to."

"It's hanging on as best it can," the doctor said. "Don't be too hard on it. Or yourself. If you're comfortable with it, I would like to discharge you tonight, so you can spend the week resting at the palace."

"And if she needs anything?"

"I can be there as quickly as possible, or she can be brought here. But I really do think that since we're in for a bit of a wait, it's best if you just go home and make yourself comfortable."

"A week?" Tabitha asked.

"Yes. Unless… If you miscarry between now and then, we will have our answer. But hopefully, things will stay stable. And when you come back we'll have good results."

Tabitha blinked hard, trying to hold back any more tears. "Okay." She took a deep breath. "Okay."

"Do you have any more questions for me?"

"That will be all," Kairos said.

Tabitha didn't have the energy to protest him making proclamations on behalf of the both of them. She closed her eyes, waiting until she heard the doctor's footsteps recede from the room.

"Are you ready?" he asked.

She swallowed hard. "I suppose so."

She stayed silent on the ride home and when he helped her walk into the palace, leading her back to her bedroom. She had not been here in over a month. It felt foreign, strange. She wished very much that she could go back to the island. Go back to earlier yesterday evening. She had felt happy. She had felt as though pieces were finally falling into place. Yes, she knew that she was still going to have to fight to claim him, but she'd been ready to do it. They'd had their fourteen days. And now it was shortened, taken from them. Now they were back here, in the palace, in the middle of reality. Facing an uncertain future. The possibility of a grief that she didn't feel prepared to handle.

It wasn't fair. She had finally gotten up the nerve to leave him, only to fall pregnant with his child. And now, after working so hard to forge a connection with him, to try and repair their marriage, she might be losing the baby.

What was the point of any of it?

She extricated herself from Kairos's firm hold, and crawled onto her soft bed, turning away from him, drawing her knees up to her chest.

"Are you all right?"

"No," she said, surprised at the strength in her response. "No, I'm not all right. This is wrong. All of it is wrong."

"I know."

"Not like I know it," she said, being petulant. Being unfair. Because it was her body that was enduring all of this uncertainty and pain. Because she was the one who cared so much that she had to walk away rather than spend a lifetime in pain, loving a man who didn't love her back.

The realization made her stomach clench tight.

She loved him. Of course she did. She was such a fool, she never even let herself think the words for fear of the deeper implications. For fear of how much pain it would cause her in the future. But it didn't make it less true.

She wanted to be sick. Realizing that she loved him now, even as the beautiful future she had begun to imagine for them slipped away. If she lost this baby, what would be left for them? More years of trying? Or would he finally be done with her?

She knew the answer. He would stay with her. He had already made that clear. It was one reason he had pushed Andres to marry Zara, because then they could provide the country with an heir.

Misery stole over her. They were going to be right back where they started. Unless he felt differently now.

"I'm very sorry that you're having to go through this," he said.

"Aren't you going through it too?" Now she was just being spiteful. He'd said that he knew. That he understood. And she had attempted to lay a bigger claim to it than he had. Now he was giving her that claim, and she was angry because he didn't seem as affected as she was.

"Of course I am," he said. "You have no idea how important this child is to me. As the ruler of the country, it has been instilled in me from birth what my responsibilities are in this role. Producing an heir is at the forefront of those responsibilities at this stage of my life."

She sat up, anger overtaking some of the weariness. "Is that the only reason it matters to you?"

"Of course not. How can you even ask me that? I have my doubts of what manner of father I'll be. My own father had an iron fist and he certainly put me on the path to being a good ruler. But in terms of being a father, and not just a drill instructor? I'm not certain he was successful on that score. I want more for our child. I want to be different. And I don't know how to give it. I'm already worried about it. I've already thought about what it would be like to hold this baby. To walk on the beach with him or her, as we did together this week. Do not insult me by asking if the throne is the only reason I care."

"It's all you talk about."

"It's the easiest thing to talk about."

Silence settled between them. She wasn't sure what to say to that. He was right. Talking about the kingdom, the throne, was much easier than discussing feelings. Fears. Much simpler than talking about the feelings that were crowding her chest, making her feel as though she couldn't breathe. Love. Stupid, terrible love that she didn't want to feel.

"This has to work," he said, his tone desperate.

Yes, it did. Because if they didn't have the baby, what did they have? Nothing more than a cold union, and no reason to try and hold it together. She felt as though she was going to have a panic attack. She couldn't breathe.

"Tabitha," he said, his tone suddenly harsh. "Are you okay? You look like you're going to pass out."

"I need to lie down."

"Yes."

She rested her head on her pillow, pulling the covers up to her chin. "Today was terrible."

"Tomorrow will be better," he said, his tone firm and distant.

"Stay with me?" She knew that she shouldn't ask. She knew that it betrayed too much. But she just wasn't in a place to protect her pride at the moment.

There was nothing but silence in place of where his answer should be. She waited. And he said nothing.

"Please," she said.

"I had better not. You need to get some rest. You do not need me taking up any of your mattress. I'll be in my room if you need me. Keep your phone by your bed, call me if necessary."

She gritted her teeth, pain, anger lashing at her. "And will you deign to answer these texts? We both know you ignore me very often."

"I promise I won't," he said, his tone like iron.

She said nothing else to him. Instead, she waited for him to leave. She closed her eyes, turning away from him, listening to his footsteps, to the sound of the door closing. Her head was swirling with too many possibilities. Too many thoughts. It was a good thing the media didn't know about the baby yet. There was no way she could handle any of this publicly, when she had no idea how to deal with it privately.

And why are you thinking about the media at a time like this?

Because that was easier than thinking about her husband.

He was already distancing himself. Truth be told, he had been even before the medical scare.

It was then she realized that for all the talking she had done about her past, he still hadn't done any talking about his own. Yes, on paper, she knew exactly what had happened during Kairos's childhood. She knew his mother had left when he was only twelve. But she didn't know how he felt about it. Didn't know how it had impacted him at the time. Or how it impacted him now. She had told him everything—about the way her stepfather had died. About why she had worked so hard to change her life.

And all the time he had listened, but he had never given her anything in return. He had quieted any thoughts and concerns with kisses, and she had let him.

Suddenly, she sat up, rolling out of bed and

walking toward her bedroom door before she could fully process what she was doing. She was tired. She was distraught. She needed to speak to Kairos.

She padded down the hall to his bedroom, which was situated right next to hers. She didn't bother to knock, rather she just opened the door. He was standing by his bed, his back facing her, his bare skin filling her vision. No, she couldn't afford to get distracted by such a thing. Anyway, right now, she was too physically tender to allow sex to cloud what was happening between them.

He turned sharply, his brows locked together. "Are you okay? You don't need to come to get me. I'll come to you. You should be lying down."

"Nothing new happened. But I was thinking. We...we need to talk, Kairos."

"Do we? I think we both need to rest."

"Of course you do. Because you don't want to talk to me. You're more than happy to allow me to talk to you. In fact, you encourage it. You don't give me anything in return."

"Do I not give you anything? You could have

fooled me. I thought I gave you quite a bit on the couch last night."

"Sex is not intimacy," she said, her voice vibrating with emotion. "It certainly can be. It has been for me. But I don't think it is for you. I think you use it to distract me. To distract yourself. I have given you so much of myself this past week. I told you about my past. I told you why I left you. What I wanted. For us, for our future. I feel like you've given me none of that in return."

"What is it you want from me, Tabitha?"

"Honesty. It's time for you to talk to me. I made the choice to trust you, Kairos, and I need you to trust me too. I need to know that we're going to have more than this distance between us."

"I can't promise that."

"Why not? You're going to have to do what I did. You're going to have to make a decision. You should be able to promise too."

"Well, I'm not going to do that. I can't."

"Why not?"

"It is not possible for me. Tabitha, I have to be strong. I have to be the king. I cannot afford to look back and examine my past. And I will not.

I cannot afford to be vulnerable. Not to you, not to anything. We will have our child, and everything will make sense. I have to confess to you now that we may never have the marriage that you want. But it is still no less than I ever promised you. I have to serve Petras first. It requires me to maintain a certain amount of distance."

"Kairos," she said, her throat closing uptight, sorrow filling her chest.

"You will not be unhappy. I think we understand each other better now. I understand you. And this… This is my honesty. It is all I can give. I am sorry if it hurts you. I truly am. But there is nothing to be done."

She nodded, swallowing hard as she turned away from him. She had tried. She had failed. She didn't know if there was anything else she could do.

"Good night," she said, walking out of the room and heading back toward hers. She closed the door firmly behind her, feeling that there was something definitive about it. About this separation. It felt very final.

No matter what, he was never going to drop

his guard. He had said it now, admitted to it. He thought everything would be fine because they would have their child, and it would give her purpose. The connection she craved. But if they didn't, then she would be left with nothing. And even if they did, there was not enough between her and Kairos to want to stay in the union. She loved him. She needed him to love her too, and nothing less.

That, she realized, was the happiness she had been searching for.

She had moved through life looking for status, looking for money, for security. But she had forged no connections. Until her marriage to Kairos. And even then, in a palace, with beautiful clothes, she had been unhappy. There was more to life than that. There was love. That was what she truly craved. No money could buy it, no title could bestow it. And she could not force Kairos to feel it for her.

She lay down on the bed, the cool sheets doing little to ease the hot thrum of anxiety rioting through her veins. She was going to have to make a decision about where to go from here. But not tonight.

Tonight she was just going to sleep. She was going to cling tightly to better thoughts of the future. She wrapped her arms around her mid-section and closed her eyes tight. She was going to cling to her baby too. Pray that she made it through the night without more bleeding. Pray that she made it through with this at least.

For the first time it was easy for her to wish that she could just stay in the present. Here in the palace, married to Kairos, such as that marriage was. Pregnant with his baby. With her baby. But no matter how much she knew these things for certain, who knew what would happen tomor-row? Who knew where she would be? She didn't have a clue.

Tears started to fall from her eyes, and she didn't bother to wipe them away. Didn't bother to keep control, or pretend it didn't hurt.

This was all because of love. And even now, she couldn't regret it. She had been afraid of this. Of hurt, of heartbreak. And still, even having the worst fear confirmed, even knowing that opening herself up would only cause her pain, she regretted nothing.

At least this was honest. At least this was real. At least she wasn't hiding.

She would rather be wounded in the light than slowly fade away in the darkness. No matter how much it hurt.

CHAPTER TWELVE

KAIROS FOUND THAT he couldn't sleep. He spent the rest of the early morning hours doing paperwork in his office, then went to the dining room for coffee and breakfast. He was shocked when he saw Tabitha sitting at the table, a mug of tea in front of her, along with a piece of toast. She was dressed impeccably, in her usual style. A pristine black dress, a single strand of pearls, her blond hair pulled back into a bun. The only indication that she had not slept well was the dark circles under her eyes.

"Are you well?" he asked, moving to the head of the table to sit down.

"I'm still pregnant, if that's what you're asking."

"Yes, that is what I was asking." Except it wasn't. He wanted to ask her how she had slept.

He wanted to ask if he had wounded her terribly last night. But he could not.

"All right, then, now that that's out of the way. There is something else we need to discuss."

"I would like to have some coffee first."

"And I don't want to wait. In this instance, I feel I should get my way. As I'm the one who is pregnant and in distress."

"I'm in a decent amount of distress, having not had any sleep or caffeine."

She shot him a pointed, deadly glare. "Why didn't you stay with me last night?"

"Because you needed rest."

"And you were going to keep me up all night, telling me ghost stories?"

"No, not ghost stories. But I may not have respected the fact that you needed rest, and not my lecherous advances."

"I have a bit more respect for your control than that, Kairos. I hardly think you're going to accost your recently hospitalized wife."

He gritted his teeth. "You don't know that. Neither do I, frankly. The way that I treated you before the bleeding started was appalling."

"On that score we can agree."

He thought back to how roughly he handled her, how desperate he'd been. He would never forgive himself if anything happened to their baby. Because of him. It would all be because of him.

"I am sorry," he said, his voice rough. "Do forgive me for how rough I was. I lost myself in a way I did not believe possible."

"What are you talking about?"

"I was too rough with you."

"That isn't what I thought you were talking about. I thought you meant after. When you left me. I was upset about that. I needed you to stay. I needed you to hold me. You had… Kairos, you had never done that to me before. It had never been like that. I needed to stay with you, to rest in that experience with you. Otherwise, it's just sex. It isn't intimacy at all."

Relief washed over him, but along with it came anger. Frustration. "I told you, intimacy is not something we can share. Not in the way you want it. You wanted honesty, and I am willing to offer.

I'm just sorry it isn't the grand revelation you were hoping for."

"I don't understand why. I still don't understand."

"I cannot make you understand," he said, his temper fraying now. "There is nothing I can say beyond what I have already said."

"Tell me something. Tell me something real about you. Tell me… Tell me what happened when your mother left. Tell me what it is like to have your father raise you."

"I have told you about my father already. He was cold, he was distant. He was trying to make me strong. And I understand why. I cannot resent him for it, even if I cannot claim to have felt happiness in my childhood. It made me the man that I am, the man that I must be."

"Stop it. You're not a robot. You're a human being. Stop pretending that you don't have any feelings. Stop pretending that a childhood being raised by a drill sergeant was fine just because it turned you into what you consider to be an ideal ruler. It's false, Kairos. It all rings so incredibly false. And I can't live a life that way anymore.

I simply can't. I spent too many years hiding. Too many years pursuing empty things, looking for happiness that I was never going to find hiding behind a wall. I was so deeply concealed I couldn't even see the sun. Yes, I didn't feel very many bad things, but I didn't feel good things either. Right now? I have never been more terrified than I am right now. I have never prayed so hard for something to work out. I want this baby more than you can imagine. And the very idea of losing it fills me with so much pain… I can barely even think of it at all. But I wouldn't trade it. Not for anything. I wouldn't go back and protect myself by never becoming pregnant. Because it's touched deeper parts of myself that I never even knew existed. It makes me hope. With a kind of intensity I didn't know I could feel. And it's the same…it's the same with you."

The back of his neck prickled, cold dread living in his chest and radiating outward. "What do you mean?"

"This can't last," she said, her tone filled with sadness, with regret.

"What can't?" he bit out.

"This. Us. I can't go back to the way things were. And if this scare with the baby has taught me anything, it's that what we tried to build on the island still isn't strong enough."

"No. That isn't true," he said, terror clawing at him now.

"It is. Because I can't fight against a brick wall. Not forever. And yes, for a while, I thought maybe it could be different. I thought maybe I could make it work for the sake of the baby. But if that's the only reason we're doing this, then we're not building a strong enough foundation. We only make each other miserable. We'll make our child miserable."

"Or, do you secretly believe you're going to lose it? Are you hoping that you will?"

He regretted his words when he saw her reaction to them. She drew back, as though he had slapped her. "Of course I don't. I want more than anything for our child to be born healthy. But, Kairos, we might lose the baby. And then why are we together? If there isn't an answer to that question, we shouldn't be together no matter what happens."

"You don't think that the heat between us is a reason to stay together?"

"No. Because it isn't enough. Because I can't get so close to what I want and then have you pull away. It's cruel. I can't exist this way, not anymore."

"Why are you changing things?" he roared, standing up from his seat, rage propelling him forward. "We had a bargain from the beginning. Are you such a liar, such a manipulative bitch?" He hated himself. Hated the words that were coming out of his mouth, but he couldn't stop them. He felt as though the floor was dropping out from beneath him. He had given her everything he was able to give her, and still it wasn't enough. Still she was leaving him. How dare she? He was the king. She was carrying his child. She was his wife.

"Because I changed. I'm sorry. I love you, Kairos. If you can't love me back—I don't mean just *saying* that you love me to make me stay— I mean showing me. I mean giving me parts of yourself. Giving me your soul, not just your body, then I can't stay. Because it hurts too badly."

He felt as though she had reached inside his chest and grabbed hold of his heart, squeezing it tight. She stood up, taking a step away from him, and he felt as if she was going to pull his heart straight from his chest now. That if she took another step away she would take it with her.

Perhaps you should be grateful if she did.

He couldn't breathe.

"Do not leave me," he said.

"What would you give me? And I don't mean clothing, or money, or even pleasure. What will you give me of yourself? Kairos, I've witnessed terrible things. Things that no child should ever have to see. I spent my life hiding because it fractured my view of people. Because for a long time I believed that everyone was hiding something dark and frightening beneath the surface. I had to choose to trust you, and it was the hardest thing I have ever done. So when you tell me that you can't give more to me, I believe you. And I'm not going to sign up for blind faith. For

going on for another five years, living in hope
that someday you might fall for me. That someday you might break down the wall you've put
up around yourself."

"I am a king. I have to put a wall around myself."

"Why?"

He didn't like these questions. Didn't like that
her words tested the logic of his argument. "Because I must," he answered. He refused to dig
deeper. Refused to uncover that dark well, the
lid to the center of his chest, the one that housed
the truth of all this. The outcome would be the
same, so there was no point. No point at all.

"And I must do this. I have to go, Kairos. I
have to."

She turned away from him and he found himself staring down his worst fear. As the woman
who rooted him to the earth, who kept his heart
beating, began to walk away from him. He had
lowered himself completely and begged for his
mother to stay, and it had made no difference.
And here he was again, facing down his fear.
He had to wonder if that moment on the beach

wasn't a cautionary tale so much as it was a pre-monition.

She kept walking away, and he said nothing.

Tell her to stay.

His entire body seized up, his throat closing. And still, he said nothing.

He watched her walk out, her shoulders straight and still. Proud in that way Tabitha always was. And so silent, even when she was hurting. Five years he'd been married to her and most of the time she'd been in pain.

Because of him.

At least this way, she's free of you.

He was free of her too. He should be grateful. He did not need a wife. Everything would be fine with the child, there was no other option. The child would be fine. He would have his heir, and the country would be secured.

That was all that mattered. There was no honor in being a divorced king, but his father had been. This country had been absent a queen for a very long time.

And so it would be again.

He laughed into the empty space, a bitter, hollow sound. He had always aspired to be the king his father was. And now, he had become so.

A king without a queen, who had surrounded his heart in a wall of stone as cold as the castle that he lived in.

Without her, it would be all the colder. But he would welcome it, embrace it. It would make him the leader he had always needed to be. It was a small sacrifice to make for the good of the nation.

A good ruler led with his head and not his heart. A good thing too. Because when Tabitha walked out, she took his heart with her.

And still, he let her leave. In the end, he counted it a blessing.

Finer feelings were for men who had not been born with a kingdom to protect.

He clenched his jaw tightly, and curled his fingers into fists, tightening his hold until his tendons ached. He welcomed the dull pain because it distracted him from the sharp, bitter anguish in his chest. An ache he had a feeling he would have to become accustomed to.

But it was nothing he had not dealt with before. He would make room for this pain next to the one left by his mother. And he would go on as he always had.

There was no other option.

CHAPTER THIRTEEN

FOR THREE NIGHTS, Kairos was plagued with nightmares. Images of a woman walking away from him, of his voice not working, his feet being stuck to the spot. He hated this. This feeling of powerlessness. And in his sleep, it refused to abate. During the day, he did what was required of him. He even issued an official statement regarding the separation of himself and the queen.

Part of him had imagined that if he took official steps to deal with the divorce, it would set things right inside of him. That it would make things feel final. But nothing took away the dreams.

He threw the covers back on his bed and stood, walking out the double doors that led to a balcony that overlooked the mountains and the forest back behind the palace. There was still snow on the ground here in Petras at the higher elevations, and it blanketed everything in glittering frost, making the time spent on the island seem even more surreal. Even more removed from time.

He was continually waiting for a sense of relief to hit. With Tabitha gone, he would not have to contend with the more conflicting elements of their relationship. He would be free to focus again with a kind of single-mindedness he hadn't fully managed since they married.

The icy air bit into his bare skin and he did nothing to shield himself from the cold as he walked farther out onto the balcony, resting his hands on the balustrade and looking out over all of the land that he bore responsibility for. This was his birthright. This was what he would leave to his child, should he ever truly have one.

Usually, he felt some sense of pride looking down at Petras. Tonight, the bare landscape seemed as empty as he was. It did not seem full of promise, at least, not for any future he cared about. He should be angry. Angry that Tabitha had proven to be as false as every other woman in his life.

But he was not. Because for whatever reason, he could not make comparisons between Tabitha and his mother, not now. Yes, that moment had reminded him of the day his mother had walked away, but she was not his mother.

And he'd never truly been afraid of that. He'd told himself he was. That he needed a cold, loveless union to prevent himself from falling prey to a fickle, passionate woman. But that had never been his real fear. *He* was his real fear.

When he had fallen to his knees and wept after his mother had left, when he had refused to leave his room, to get out of bed for days after she had gone, his father had told him that he showed the same signs of weakness that had caused his mother to abandon her duty.

And Kairos had known it to be so. After their mother had left, many people looked at Andres and thought that he was a reflection of the queen. Flighty, free-spirited, and given to reckless, spontaneous action. But Kairos had known the truth.

Andres—while giving the impression of being the feckless spare—did everything with a measure of cold calculation. He did it for the response of the people around him, did it to test their loyalty. And he did it to great effect. But it was Kairos who had that deep well of emotion down in his soul. The one that he could not control. The one that would cause him to act recklessly, to abandon his duty if emotion dictated.

He had wanted to be his father. Desperately. To be the kind of leader that the country needed. But he had known that he wasn't. He was his mother, through and through. Weak, emotional. And so, he had sought to destroy it. To go out of his way to erect barriers between those deadly emotions and his decisions. So he had trapped both himself and Tabitha in a union that could have been, and should have been so much more than he was willing to allow it to be.

Because he was afraid. Afraid of what he might do. Afraid of how weak he might truly be.

You just have to choose. You have to choose to trust.

No. He could not make that choice. Couldn't choose to trust himself or Tabitha.

He gritted his teeth against the anguish that assaulted him. He wanted her. Just thinking about her sent a wave of longing over him. A wave of longing that was destined to go unmet for the rest of his life.

He thought back again to the night his mother had left. To the look in her eyes. Sadness. Fear. She had been afraid. He had never fully realized that before this moment. How could he? When she had left, he had been little more than a boy, concerned entirely with his own emotions and not at all with hers. She was the enemy of that tale, and nothing more. That had been reinforced by his father, and also by his increased understanding of the way she had treated Andres when he was a boy.

But, for some reason, now all he could see was the fear. It twisted the memory, changed it. Made the moment into something different altogether. She wasn't walking away from him. She was running. Running from the palace. From that life. Likely, from the weight of responsibility.

Oh, how he knew that fear. That very same fear. He was running, even now.

He turned away from the balustrade, walking back into the bedroom, and pulled on his pants. Then he took a sharp breath and walked out the door, stalking down the hall, headed for his office. He badly needed a drink. Something, anything to quiet the demons that were rioting through his mind.

He pushed open the door, making his way to the bar at the far end of the room, shutting out all of the memories currently assaulting him of what it had been like to take Tabitha in here. To put her up on that desk and release five years of desperate sexual tension in one heady moment.

He ignored the images that were assuming control of his consciousness and poured a measure of liquor into a glass. Behind him, he heard the door open. He turned, part of him expecting to see Tabitha there for some strange reason.

But no. Tabitha was gone. And it was only Andres.

"What are you doing up?" Kairos asked.

"I got up to ask you that question. It isn't every day I see you wandering around the palace without a shirt. Actually, it isn't any day." Andres walked into the room, over toward the bar. He took the whiskey bottle out of Kairos's hand and set about to pouring himself a generous portion. "Do you want to talk about it?"

"I would rather be publicly flogged, then tarred in honey and rolled over an anthill."

"Excellent. Pretend that I didn't ask, but that I'm commanding we talk about it instead."

"Excuse me, Andres. If you have forgotten you are the spare? I am your king."

Andres waved a hand. "All hail." He took a sip of his drink. "Does this have something to do with your wife?"

He looked down at his glass. "She left."

"Right. This is after your last-ditch reconciliation attempt of the past week and a half or so."

"Yes."

"I hate to be the one to tell you this, Kairos, but that is not how a reconciliation is supposed to work."

"I'm not in an exceptionally good mood, Andres. So unless you want to find yourself in the…stocks or something, you might want to watch the way you speak to me."

"I don't know what century you're living in, but there are no stocks in the town square anymore."

"I might be tempted to build some."

"Tell me what's happening," Andres said, all teasing gone from his tone now. "It can't end like this between the two of you."

"Why not?"

"Because you love her. And I know she sure as hell loves you, though I can't quite figure out why."

Kairos lifted the glass to his lips, trying not to betray just how frightening he found Andres's words. "She said she loved me."

"I see," Andres said. "As one who nearly destroyed his own chance at happiness, take my advice. If a woman like that loves you, then you would be a fool to refuse her." Andres paused for a moment. "Actually, it's very close to advice you gave me. You told me that if Tabitha looked at you the way that Zara looked at me, you would never let her go. But she does, Kairos. She always has. I know you don't find emotion easy. I certainly don't, or haven't, in the past. But that doesn't mean it isn't worth it."

"What did you think of our father, Andres?"

Andres frowned. "I don't know. He didn't have

very much time for me. I wasn't of any great value to him."

"And our mother?"

"You know she had no patience for me," Andres said, speaking of how she used to leave him at home during royal events. Afraid that he would cause a scene, that he would somehow find a way to sabotage things.

"Did you ever...? Did you ever wonder why?"

Andres laughed, a short, bitter sound. "Well, as it's the source of all of my emotional issues, I have wondered a time or two."

"They have much to answer for, our parents," Kairos said.

"As do I," Andres said. "Have I ever told you, with all sincerity, how sorry I am about what happened with Francesca? Because I am. Very sorry."

"I know," Kairos said. "And to be honest with you...I was only ever relieved. It was never her for me. Never."

"That doesn't excuse me. Neither does our mother's exit. I know it wasn't only me. But I did blame myself. Now, I understand that there must have been other things happening. I just don't know what."

Kairos nodded slowly. "Yes. I was there. The night that she left. I tried to—I tried to stop her. Looking back, I feel like she seemed afraid."

"It's strange you should say that. What I think of her now, that's what I think. She didn't seem so much angry at me, as afraid of...something."

"Did you ever want to find her?"

"No one knows what happened to her."

"No," Kairos said, his voice broken. "That isn't true."

"Kairos?"

"I know where she is," Kairos said. "I have known. I went searching for her after our father died. Or rather, I had someone do a bit of searching. I haven't made contact. But I do know that she's living in Greece, using a different name."

"I don't think I want to speak to her," Andres said.

"And I don't blame you. Not with the way she treated you. But I...I might need to."

"You do what you have to. But I may not be able to support you with this."

"Tabitha's pregnant," he said. He had been determined not to tell his brother, particularly as everything was in a precarious position at the moment, but he found he couldn't hold back any longer. He needed Andres to understand why he was going to pursue contact with their mother. Especially after all she had put his brother through. "It isn't going well. The doctor's concerned that she will miscarry. But she is pregnant, for now."

Andres cursed. "I…I'm not entirely certain what to say to that. Whether or not to congratulate you."

"It's difficult. That's why…that's why I tried to save our marriage."

"Is that the only reason?"

"No. Of course not."

"Did you tell her that?"

"I don't know what to tell her. I don't…I don't know how to do this. I spent too many years training myself not to feel things. I don't recognize any of it now. I don't know how to move forward now."

Andres nodded slowly. "I think you're lying to

yourself. I think you know full well how to pro-ceed. I think you know full well how you feel. I just think that you also happen to be terrified."

Kairos couldn't argue with that. "That's why I need to talk to our mother. I have to find some-thing out."

"And you don't think you'll give the poor woman a stroke? Calling her after twenty years of no contact?"

"Well, I think she nearly gave me one when she left me crying on the palace floor as a twelve-year-old boy. We can consider ourselves even."

"I thought I was a little bit more well-adjusted since my marriage, but all of this emotion still makes me slightly uncomfortable."

"Extremely."

"Do whatever you have to do, Kairos, but do not let Tabitha get away." Andres turned and walked out of the office, leaving Kairos alone.

Now, all he had to do was wait until it was late enough for him to call a woman he hadn't seen in more than two decades.

He was afraid. He didn't know if he could trust her, or himself.

But if he had learned one thing from Tabitha it was that you had to make choices. And he was making them now.

"Hello. Is this Maria?" Kairos could scarcely breathe around the lump in his throat as he waited for the response to come down the telephone line.

"Yes," the response came, questioning, uncertain.

"Then I am hoping I've reached the right person. It is entirely possible I have not. But I am King Kairos of Petras. And if that means anything to you, then you are the person I'm looking for."

There was nothing in response to that but silence, and for a moment, Kairos was certain she had hung up the phone.

"Hello?" he asked.

"I'm here," she said. "I'm here."

"You are my mother."

"Yes," she said, her voice a whisper.

"I am very sorry to call you suddenly like this. Especially because I do not have time to make light conversation. There are some things I need to know. And it may be difficult."

"You don't have to apologize to me. I'm the one who should be apologizing."

"Perhaps," he said, ignoring the knot that tightened in his chest. "But there will be plenty of time for that. Later."

"I hope so. What is it you need to know, Kairos?" she asked, her voice wrapping itself around his name like an embrace.

"I need to understand why you left. And I need to know why... I need to know why you treated Andres as you did. He will not ask."

"He grew up to be quite a lot of trouble, didn't he?" The question wasn't full of judgment, but rather a soft, sad sort of affection.

"You have read the tabloids, I take it?"

"Some. I could never resist the chance to look upon you again. Even if only for a moment."

"He has settled. He has a wife. He is a good husband to her. Where I fear...I am not so accomplished as a spouse." He took a deep breath. "This is why I need to know. I need to know why you left."

"It took me a very long time to answer that question for myself," she said, her voice sounding thin. "A lot of therapy. A lot of regrets. Please, know that I regretted it. Even as I was leaving. But there was no going back."

"My father's doing?"

"Yes. He could not… He said he could not forgive me. And that the damage was already done. It wasn't only that he refused to take me back… he refused to let me see you."

It didn't surprise him to hear that about his father. And perhaps, because it was so unsurprising, he couldn't find it in him to be angry. He only felt a strange sense of relief over the fact that she had thought of them again. She had wanted to come back. Selfish, perhaps. But he found comfort in it.

"I knew it would come to that point with him," she continued, her voice sad. "I always had. My family raised me to be the queen. To marry the king. I was trained. But I always feared that I would not be equal to the task. Your father would get so angry when Andres would act up. That's why I stopped having him come to events. I was afraid he would start taking it out on him. As it was, he simply took it out on me."

"He didn't hurt you?"

"Not physically. But…it was very trying. I was afraid of where it might lead eventually. I was just so afraid of doing something wrong. And you boys were a reflection on me. In your father's eyes, if you did something wrong, it was directly related to a weakness of mine. And I…I wasn't strong enough to fight against that. I was so low. And I just left you with him. That was the hardest thing later. Once I was gone. Realizing that I had abandoned you to stay with that cold man who… But I didn't feel I was helping you. Not by being there. I certainly wasn't helping Andres. I couldn't be the mother that he needed. I did more harm to him than I ever did good. Once I realized that…I just…I didn't feel I did a good enough job as queen. And I didn't feel I did a good enough job as a mother. At that point, I had convinced myself that you were better off without me. I was just so afraid that if I didn't leave, he would make me go. And for some reason, that seemed worse. And if I waited for that…well, I might have done more damage to you both by then and I was so afraid of that."

Kairos nodded, before realizing that she couldn't see him. "Yes," he said, his voice rough, "I can understand that."

"You can?" she asked, her voice so filled with hope it broke his heart.

"Yes. I have been afraid too. But someone very wise once told me that sometimes we just have to make a choice. A choice to trust. The choice to let go."

He realized, right then, that he had a choice to make. To release his hold on the past, to refuse to allow any more power over the present. Tabitha was right. You couldn't wait for these things to go away. Couldn't wait until a magical moment of certainty, couldn't wait for a guarantee. It didn't exist.

There was no magic. Sometimes, you had to get up and move the mountains all on your own.

"That is very wise. But I'm not certain I deserve for anyone to choose to let my sins go."

"I'm not certain that matters either," he said. There were so many years between this moment, and that moment in the hall in the palace when his mother had left. So much bitterness. So much pain. Part of him railed against the idea of releasing it, because shortly, it couldn't be so simple.

In truth, he knew it wouldn't be simple. But it was the only way forward.

"Come and visit us," he said. "When you can. The palace will facilitate your travels."

"Oh," she said. "Are you… You're certain you want to see me?"

"You left because of fear. I pushed my wife away because I was afraid. There is nothing more to fear now. Anger, hurt, it doesn't have to stand in the way. At least, not if we make the choice to put it away."

"You would do that for me?"

"For me. For me, first. Don't get the idea that I turned into anything too selfless. I realized that I had to speak to you, to put all of this to rest first before I could move on with my life. I want very much for us to get on with life. All of us."

"I would very much like that too, though I don't deserve it."

"Heaven forbid we only got what we deserved.

If that were the case, then there would be no point in me going and trying to fix things with Tabitha," he said.

"Go. You should always go. I didn't. And I will never stop regretting it."

"No more regrets. For any of us."

CHAPTER FOURTEEN

TABITHA FELT WRUNG OUT. She hadn't had the energy to try and secure herself a place other than Kairos's penthouse, and to his credit, he hadn't come after her. Also, to his discredit, he hadn't come after her. She didn't know what she wanted. She didn't know what she had expected. Something. To hear from him.

You expected him to stop you.

Yes, two days ago when she had walked out of the palace, she had expected him to prevent her from leaving. But he hadn't. He had simply let her go. Damned contrary man.

The bright spot was that she had no more bleeding. She was feeling well, and not terribly drained. At least, not physically. Emotionally, she felt exhausted. She was sad. As though there was a weight in each of her limbs, pulling her down, trying to bury her beneath the earth. She was beginning to think it might succeed. That the weight would win. That the overwhelming heaviness would become too great a burden, that she would simply lay her head down and not get up and spend the rest of her days in bed, watching life go by.

Why did she have to love him so much? It was more convenient when she believed herself simply unhappy because of distance. Not unhappy because she was the victim of unrequited love.

She walked out of the bedroom, into the kitchen, feeling extremely contrary, because she wanted to lie down desperately, but she also needed to get something to eat. She stopped as soon as she walked into the main part of the room. She pressed her hand to her chest, as if it would keep her heart from beating right out of it.

"Kairos," she said, stopping cold when she saw her husband standing there.

He looked as if he hadn't slept in the past two days. His black hair was disheveled and there were dark circles under his eyes. His white dress shirt was undone at the collar, the sleeves pushed up to his elbows. He looked devilish and devastating. Like every good dream she could hope to have for the rest of her life. So close, so real, but untouchable.

"Are you all right?"

"Is that going to be the first question you ask me every time we see each other from now on?" And she realized just then that they would see each other again. At least, if all went right with the pregnancy, which she desperately wanted.

They would be forced to see each other at sonograms. At the hospital when she went into labor. Every time they passed their child back and forth. She would have to watch him walk away, taking a piece of her heart with him. Not just because he was holding their child, but because he was leaving too.

There would be no clean break, no getting over it. And if he remarried… If he had more children with another woman… She would be forced to see that too. And photographs of it in the papers, and clips of it on TV. A woman standing in her position.

She pressed her hand to her stomach, and doubled over, a harsh cry escaping her lips.

"Tabitha!" Suddenly, his strong arms were around her, holding her close. "Tabitha, what is it?"

"I can't do this," she said, her voice nearly a sob. "How can I see you and not have you? How can I watch you with another woman? How can I watch her take my place, and hold my child and bear more of yours? Kairos, this can't be endured. I can't."

"You're the one who left," he said.

"Yes, I left. Because I can't live with you when you don't love me either. Why do you have to make everything impossible?" She straightened, and he took a step back, but she followed the motion, pressing herself against his chest, hitting him with her closed fist, even while she rested her head there, listening to the sound of his beating heart. "Why do I still love you?"

"I never quite understood why you loved me in the first place," he said, his deep voice making his chest vibrate against her cheek.

"I don't either. I was very careful. I was supposed to marry a man so cold he could never melt the walls I built up. You didn't hide it well enough."

"What?"

"How wonderful you are. Even when I couldn't see it, I could feel that it was there. And I just wanted…I want everything you hide from me."

"I want to stop hiding," he said, his voice rough.

She lifted her head, looked into his dark eyes. "You what?"

"I called my mother. And I…I have to tell you something. I never wanted to tell you about the night my mother left. It was a defining moment for me. A mark of my great failure, a warning against what I might become. My greatest weakness."

"You aren't weak. If there's one thing I know about you, Kairos, it's that."

"But I have been. Just not…in the way that I recognized weakness. I have been afraid. Like you, I've been afraid of being hurt again. Afraid of undoing everything I have learned. And that if it happens, I will no longer be able to do what I need to do as king of this country. It isn't that I feel nothing, Tabitha. I feel things, so deeply, and I spent a great many years trying to train that away."

"What happened when your mother left?"

"I saw her. I saw her walking out and I knew. I knew because I always felt I was more like her than I was like my father. She felt things so deeply. At first, it was one of the very beautiful things about her. But I... Talking to her, I understand. My father took that softness and twisted it. He made her feel like there was something wrong with her. Like her feelings were going to bring down the kingdom. I understand, because he did the same with me. He saw me crying after she left. I started the moment I fell to my knees and begged her to stay, and she walked out anyway. And I didn't stop. He saw me, twelve years old and weeping like a baby for my mama, and he told me that I could not afford such emotion. Such weakness. But you see, it is this false strength that has become my greatest enemy. It has kept me safe from heartbreak, but it has destroyed any chance I might have had at a normal life. At love. And when you told me you loved me…I didn't know how to respond. Or, rather, I didn't know how to be brave enough to respond."

"Kairos, of course you're brave. You're the strongest man I've ever known."

"Who was reduced to trembling by your declaration."

"Love is terrifying. It's certainly the most terrifying thing I've ever confronted."

"But everything of value comes at a price, does it not? Otherwise it would have no value. And so, I think the price for love is that you must lay down your fear. Your anger. Your resentment. Because you cannot carry them and carry love along with them. But no one can put them down for you. And very often, time is not enough to reduce the burden. So you must set them down. As you said, for you, trust had to be a choice. You chose to trust me, and I used it badly. For that, I am sorry."

"I was going to say that's okay. But it really isn't. You hurt me. So badly."

"I know." He reached up, cupping her cheek. "I know. Tabitha, my arms are empty now. I set everything down. Everything that will get in the way of you. Of the love that I want to give you." He wrapped his arms around her, pulling her into his embrace. "I put it all away so that I could carry my love for you. It's all I want. It's all I need."

Her heart was thundering hard, her throat tight, aching. She could hardly believe the words she was hearing. She was afraid for a moment that she might be dreaming. "You love me?"

"I have. From the beginning. But there was too much in the way. Too many things I didn't need. All I need, all I have ever needed, is you. You make me a stronger man. My love for you is what makes me think that I should be."

"We don't even know… Kairos, if I lose this baby, I don't know if there will ever be another one." She swallowed hard. "Five years, it took five years for us to conceive this one and now…"

"It doesn't matter. It…it matters, because of course I want to have children with you. But as far as whether or not I stay with you, there is no condition placed upon your ability to bear children. The country will do just fine with Andres's children if need be. Or with the children of the distant cousin if we must. The country will survive, that much I know. But I will not survive without you."

She tilted her head up, pressed a kiss to his lips. "I love you," she said, her heart so full it could burst.

"I love you too. Whatever lies ahead, we will face it together." He took hold of her hand, curled his fingers around it and pulled it against his chest, placing it right over his beating heart. "I am stronger because of you," he repeated. "Never forget that. You're the one who showed me that we always have a choice. That you can choose to let go of the painful things in the past, so that you can have a future."

"I'm so busy being happy, I realized that for myself," she said. "Because I'm so glad that now, no matter what our pasts, we're going to have a future together."

"Yes, my love, we will."

"I'm so glad, *agape*," she said, smiling up at him.

"I imagine I'm allowed to call you that again."

"Yes, because now I know you mean it."

* * *

"Do you see it?"

"What?" Tabitha asked, holding on to Kairos's hand so tightly it hurt.

"That little flicker there." Kairos pointed that out on the sonogram monitor, and they both looked at the doctor.

"You have a heartbeat," she said, smiling at Tabitha. She moved the wanderer over Tabitha's stomach, and a slight frown creased her brow. "Actually, I see another one."

All of the breath left Tabitha's lungs in a gust. "Two?"

"Yes." The doctor paused, highlighting two different places on the screen. "There," she said, pointing, "and there."

"What does that mean?" Tabitha asked, knowing that she was feeling sick. But for the past week she had been certain they would find a living baby inside of her. She could hardly process what they were seeing now.

"Twins," the doctor said.

Tabitha looked up at Kairos, who was looking a bit pale and shell-shocked. "It looks like you'll be getting your heir and spare all in one shot," Tabitha said.

"Neither of them will be a spare," Kairos said, his tone fierce.

"Of course not. But that is what they call it. And it's what you call your brother."

"I'm going to outlaw the term," he said, his eyes glued to the screen. "Twins. You're absolutely certain?"

"Completely," the doctor said. "It's very likely the bleeding was nothing, and she was simply too early in her pregnancy last week to see a heartbeat."

"Well," Kairos said, bending down and kissing her cheek. "You are certainly full of surprises, my queen."

"Quite literally, at the moment."

Kairos laughed. "Yes. Very much."

Tabitha sighed happily, her eyes on the screen, on the evidence of life in front of her. "I'm glad you put all your burdens down, Kairos."

"Is that so?"

"Yes. Because for the next eighteen years we're definitely going to have our hands full."

EPILOGUE

NEW YEAR'S EVE was officially Kairos's favorite holiday. It had been for the past five years. Ever since that New Year's Eve when his wife had been waiting in his office at midnight, ready to demand a divorce.

Because since then, everything had changed. Most importantly, he had changed.

He looked around the large family area in the palace. Everything was still decorated for Christmas, the massive tree in the corner glittering. This was the last night they would have it. The last night before all of the holiday magic was removed and everything returned back to normal.

The children were already protesting. The twins, along with Zara and Andres's brood—which was in Kairos's estimation a bit much at three, with one on the way—were not ready for the holidays to be over.

"I don't want to go to bed," Christiana said, pouting in that way of hers that was both aggravating and irresistibly charming. At four, she had discovered that she could use her cuteness against her parents to great effect.

"I don't either," said Cyrena, turning an identical pout his direction.

"It is nearly midnight," he said.

"It is not," Christiana said.

"Well," Tabitha responded, "it is somewhere in the world."

Andres laughed. "That isn't good enough," he said, "not for my niece. She's far too clever for that."

"Worry about your own children, Andres," Kairos said.

"Mine do not know their numbers yet. I live in fear of that day."

"And when they learn to spell," Zara said, placing her hand over her rounded stomach.

"The horror," Kairos said. "Okay, girls. It is truly bedtime. But I am certain if you ask her very nicely, Grandma Maria would love to come and read to you."

His mother smiled at all of them from her position on the couch. Reconciliation was never easy. It had been particularly difficult for Andres. And as far as Kairos went, it came and went like the tide for the first year or so, as he dealt with anger, sadness at all the missed years and then determination not to miss any more because of mistakes that were long past the point of correcting.

All they could do was move forward now. And now, when he saw his mother with his children, with Andres and Zara's children, he knew that none of them regretted their decision to release their hold on the past.

"Of course I will," she said. "I never tire of reading to them."

She ushered the children out of the room, and then Andres looked at Zara. "Are you exhausted yet, princess?"

"Very," she said, "and my feet hurt."

"Well, we can go back up to my bedroom, and I will rub your feet. And possibly some other things."

Zara smacked him on the shoulder, then followed him out of the room anyway, leaving Kairos and Tabitha alone.

It was then that Tabitha turned to him, smiling at him, unreserved, unrestrained. Perfection. "Do you think we'll make it until midnight tonight?"

"I do always try to stay awake until midnight on New Year's Eve. Just in case you decide to ask for a divorce. I would hate to sleep through it."

She laughed. "Not a chance." She looked around the room. "Can you imagine if we had given up then? Can you imagine what we would have missed?"

"I don't like to. I'm so grateful that you gave me a second chance."

"So am I." She leaned against him, wrapping her arm around his waist. "Do you remember when I told you how hard it was for me to be happy in the present? How difficult it is for me to simply be in the moment?"

"Yes," he said.

"It isn't now. I have lived in a million perfect moments since you said you loved me. And this is one of them."

Kairos looked around at the Christmas decorations, the evergreen twisted around the pillars, the large tree and the clear lights that glittered in the midst of the dark branches. And he had to agree. The perfect moment, the perfect woman.

The perfect life.

* * * * *

If you enjoyed this story, don't miss
the first instalment of the thrilling
PRINCES OF PETRAS *duet:*
A CHRISTMAS VOW OF SEDUCTION

MILLS & BOON®
Large Print – May 2016

The Queen's New Year Secret
Maisey Yates

Wearing the De Angelis Ring
Cathy Williams

The Cost of the Forbidden
Carol Marinelli

Mistress of His Revenge
Chantelle Shaw

Theseus Discovers His Heir
Michelle Smart

The Marriage He Must Keep
Dani Collins

Awakening the Ravensdale Heiress
Melanie Milburne

His Princess of Convenience
Rebecca Winters

Holiday with the Millionaire
Scarlet Wilson

The Husband She'd Never Met
Barbara Hannay

Unlocking Her Boss's Heart
Christy McKellen

MILLS & BOON®
Large Print – June 2016

Leonetti's Housekeeper Bride
Lynne Graham

The Surprise De Angelis Baby
Cathy Williams

Castelli's Virgin Widow
Caitlin Crews

The Consequence He Must Claim
Dani Collins

Helios Crowns His Mistress
Michelle Smart

Illicit Night with the Greek
Susanna Carr

The Sheikh's Pregnant Prisoner
Tara Pammi

Saved by the CEO
Barbara Wallace

Pregnant with a Royal Baby!
Susan Meier

A Deal to Mend Their Marriage
Michelle Douglas

Swept into the Rich Man's World
Katrina Cudmore

0516 Rom LP

MILLS & BOON®

Why shop at millsandboon.co.uk?

Each year, thousands of romance readers find their perfect read at millsandboon.co.uk. That's because we're passionate about bringing you the very best romantic fiction. Here are some of the advantages of shopping at www.millsandboon.co.uk:

* **Get new books first**—you'll be able to buy your favourite books one month before they hit the shops

* **Get exclusive discounts**—you'll also be able to buy our specially created monthly collections, with up to 50% off the RRP

* **Find your favourite authors**—latest news, interviews and new releases for all your favourite authors and series on our website, plus ideas for what to try next

* **Join in**—once you've bought your favourite books, don't forget to register with us to rate, review and join in the discussions

Visit **www.millsandboon.co.uk**
for all this and more today!